S0-BCT-640

Don Mattera

The Storyteller

JUSTIFIED PRESS

Justified Press
A division of
Ashanti Publishing (Pty) Ltd.
P.O. Box 10021
Rivonia 2128

First published 1991

ISBN 0 947451 16 1

Typeset by GraphicSet

Printed and bound by Creda Press

To the San and Khoikhoi
people of Africa, and to
their history and survival . . .

And to my many friends
in Sweden who gave me
a brief taste of freedom
and human dignity and respect
during my six months' stay
in their beautiful country.

Six of the stories in this
collection were written
in a flat in Stockholm.

Contents

Execution ... 1
Oggzee ... 21
The Uniform ... 37
Child of Ghamt-Ghareb ... 53
Die Bushie is Dood... ... 79
Death can follow a man ... 85
The Storyteller ... 99
Afrika Road ... 121

EXECUTION

I have no name.
I am every man.
I live everywhere.
I die every day.

The sun rises strong and yellow and with a brilliance I have not seen before. I realise now that there is a Presence with me in the cell. It fills me with courage and foritude in the conviction that my actions were justified. That all the terror and torture I have suffered and my determination not to break or call for mercy, underscores that justification. My persecutors will remember me for a long time. It is strangely paradoxical that these first rays of light also herald the darkest hour of my brief thirty-four years on this earth. Years lived with lightning speed and a precocious maturity in educational achievement, in politics and in the military.

Last night — from the time they brought food and clean clothes — I was in a state of insane anguish trying desperately to cling to my pride and dignity, which the usurpers had tried to destroy. It was a profoundly restless night with the wind beating wildly against the huge barred window with its black-painted frame. The judge's words keep echoing in my mind: 'Guilty as charged — treason, conspiracy to commit murder, several counts of murder and sedition. Seven death sentences to be executed as one...'

A man can die only once.

My comrades, those who had survived the brutality of interrogation and torture, were summarily tried and executed as a group after only a week of trial. They were older, senior officials in the deposed military and government. Two women were also executed after they were raped. I could hear their screams coming from across the long, high barbed wire wall where the women insurrectionists are kept.

Women prisoners have a way of screaming — like quails, their eyes gouged out, tied into nets in order to attract other quails with their plaintive anguished wailing that seeps into the marrow and pulls the heart with a sense of useless anger. One of them shouted: 'Let me see my children before I die! My children please, please!' I do not know whether her wish was granted but her pleading voice haunts me as I await my end. I feel a clutching pain as I think of my son G. How I long to see and touch his face. It is too late for me to make up for all the lost years I have spent away from him. I can understand now why people at the hour of death want to see their loved ones one last time. The screaming continues as I hear the sound of jackboots against the cement floor, booming thunder from the first to the familiar sixteenth step across my cell. Thunder coming slow and sure. Outside the sun gains confidence and flings its gift of warmth into my cell. It has seen darker days and still triumphed — morning comes confident and unafraid.

Would that I were the sun.

The three visions I have had about being freed a second time now lie subdued in the mists of my anxiety. The majestic sun cuts a path in the sky and a lone seagull flies into the sheen and is bathed in a golden liquid — its wings poised and firm as it plunges into the sea behind the grey prison walls.

Would that I were a seagull.

The last supper they gave me — fried chicken, roast potatoes, three small carrots and one hundred and two peas in a tablespoon of gravy — all present and accounted for, look up at me from the plastic plate. I spared them from being sacrificed with me. Besides I refuse to die on a full stomach. The jackboots end their long pilgrimage at step number sixteen.

As the key enters the door I think suddenly of my first experience of lovemaking so many lifetimes ago, it seems. When I shared the secrets of a strength that had lifted me to the warmth of a purging fire, and then left me spent against the supple rocks of M's body.

Centuries ago, it seems.

M and I — both twenty years old at the time — had walked from the lecture room of the university where we were reading for our degrees in political science and international law. Through the long corridor then down the sixty steps and finally into the lawned grounds we walked in silence, fearing yet excited by the thing we had set our minds to do. We crossed the bridge into the park and entered the massive orange grove where we had been meeting secretly for more than two years. No words had passed between us, for we had decided to learn the one secret of life that our parents — and the rest of mankind it seemed — had warned us against.

The risks were stark and dangerous. M spoke first:

'Do you love me?'

'Is it important?'

'Yes it is important for me to know. Can you understand that?'

'I think I do. Would it help if I told you that it is only you among those many girls in the class that I look at; only you make me feel warm inside.'

'Thank you....'

A language of innocence which ended our virginity among the orange trees. Several months later M informed me of her pregnancy. Her studies were terminated by her parents and she was sent out of the country.

She did not communicate and I never saw her again. Ah, the body of M, in the secluded love-nest when I turned the key into the door of her being and entered a new and far country. How her eyes had widened and blinked in the heat and ecstasy of our journey. Moving deeper, searching, scanning and aflame, we reached the mountain. Fulfilled and bloodied.

M and I were from different tribes or castes or classes— call it what you will — and forbidden by the customs and traditions of our different families from socialising, let alone living together or marrying. These were some of the many issues I had openly objected to and challenged as a student, and I always found myself in deep waters of conflict with my father and the Church.

The prison key turns slowly and with a malice I will take with me to the gallows. My insides shiver and the memory of M is eclipsed by the sound of the key's penetration into the door — awakening once more the embryo of a fear I had fought so desperately to silence. I look at the chicken and feel a deep remorse for its twisted and roasted frame.

Its blood is on my hands.

The heavy steel door swings open. The time has finally come. Decisive and punctual. Just like it came for the chicken, and I find cold comfort in the fact that my blood — so many times thicker than that of the chicken, will also be on someone else's gloved hands. Thick and indelible, or so I want to believe. No words pass between my executioners and me. As soldiers we know and understand the rigid disciplines. Orders are orders — even to the point of concealing the glints of familiarity and of once warm comradeship under a single flag, and in the same uniform.

I, more than anyone else, knew the rules and risks inherent in insurrection and sedition. As a high-ranking officer, the youngest to receive the Star of Courage medallion, I had challenged and transgressed the code, the flag and the uniform. They had not. The issues were as clear-cut as life and death.

I chose death.

Simple.

As for the chicken, it had had no choice in the matter of its execution. The sunlight pours hot and accusingly into the faces of my executioners and one of them lifts a gloved hand to shield his eyes against the sun's attack. I imagine him lifting an axe and I think of Marie Antoinette and her royal lover Louis. Soon I too will be history.

A silent and solid guard of honour — one in front, two on each side and one bringing up the rear, lead me to the scaffold. The tall, pock-marked one in front is the senior officer and he turns round to face the Ice Man behind. His eyes blink an instruction. The Ice Man nods and feels the rope against my wrists and nods a second time. I think of God and the prophets — how did they communicate? Clouds I could not see suddenly blot the sun from sight and tiny invisible icicles of fear roll down my back and enter between my buttocks and private parts. I shudder and contract all the muscles in that sacred region of my body. Fear really settles in and God and the prophets become dark and distant thoughts. Impotent as they are distant. I am walking the last mile of the way — to quote a line from a Christian hymn.

The bodies of two strangers — their hands tied behind their backs as mine are, hang from a scaffold ahead of us. Their navy blue or purple tongues — I can't discern the exact colour — jut derisively from their mouths. Like naughty schoolboys teasing death and having the last laugh. I can't help thinking that they chose to eat their chicken and for the fun of it, asked for second helpings.

I demanded my martyrdom in front of a firing squad, and without the traditional blindfold. I wanted to face my killers; look them in the eyes. Orders or no orders, I wanted them to flinch when they pulled the triggers. If not all, then one of them at least. But it was not to be — ropes don't spill blood.

Even my last request is turned down.

Without warning I stop dead in my tracks to scrutinise the faces of the silent strangers in the hope they will reveal something of their lost lives. My rearguard, the Ice Man, walks straight into me so that I stumble and fall to the ground, badly bruising my left cheek as well as my two big toes. A cold frown settles into his forehead and his jaws lock to produce a swollen vein which divides his craggy face. There is nothing in the rule book about sudden stops en route to the scaffold.

The senior officer stops mechanically and turns to look at me. His beady, black eyes scan the extent of my injuries and with a slight, almost imperceptible nod, he blinks twice, at me and at the Ice Man, with the authority of rank. A silent language, understood and obeyed. I am lifted to my feet and I rub the bleeding cheek against my left shoulder; the toes against the trousers. The senior officer blinks again. I decipher the intended empathy and move the sides of my mouth into a fraction of a grin. A blink and a grin. Two tiny movements, and an ocean of unspoken words flows between the shores of our hearts in my final walk to oblivion.

I think of my father and the words we could have said to each other but did not dare — firm and stubborn in our different worlds, each in his own understanding and interpretations of those far-flung continents.

A great divide that was created by the severity of sombre customs, ethnic pride and crass traditions, and the conflicts between religion and Marxism. Irreconcilable differences that had fenced off our lives. And yet how, during these three months of physical and mental torment — almost to breaking point — I had poured out my love and my life to him. Emptying myself of all those bitter years of silence, aggravated by our refusal to reach out to one another. My letters from death row — although sharply unrepentant and uncompromising — were long and emotional, seeking more his love than his forgiveness and acceptance.

My words return to me now — coming as they are from a deep part of my heart. A hollow from which have been gouged out all my entrails and feelings. I had desired my father to know how fervently I loved him before the rope was placed around my neck. But I suppose that my last letter may have caused more ill than good to our already confirmed estrangement. My letter read:

> This is my last letter. You failed to respond to all the previous ones although I had pleaded for some small intimation, a few words which would have assured me of your love. I know as sure as I am going to die, that my mother loves me. Her silence I can accept because it comes from a reverent respect and obedience to

> you. 'Your father's will be done,' she always said whenever I questioned her frail servility. Yes, your will be done on earth as it is in heaven. How shallow those words rang out through your gold fillings. Shining words. Shiny and empty. If the will of men such as you must also be done in heaven, then expect uprisings and sedition there as well.

My thoughts are stirred by the sudden flight of pigeons from the roof of the women's cells. A woman is singing a song I sang as a young boy. Now there is something in a woman's voice that can permeate the air and fill the senses with an indescribable joy — as did my mother's when she sang to me. How I loved her soothing and melodic tone. Soft and velvety and with a sustenance that only mothers exude and possess. Yet as the years went by she was forced by my father's unyielding conservatism and religious orthodoxy to mask her strength. That last letter reminded him of this:

> I am aware that you will dismiss this declaration of my love for you because I have not confessed my contrition for my so-called crimes against the usurpers and your Church. But I cannot submit. To do so would negate our cause and be a betrayal of my comrades who have already paid the ultimate price. More than anything, it would be a personal betrayal. So many children, armed only with stones and dustbin lids, and a firm faith in their struggle, fought against your regime and were butchered. No lines were drawn. No quarter given. Blood and flames still ravage the nation and thousands have died. NO! To submit would be a death worse than hanging....

I feel the Ice Man's knee against the back of my thigh. His two young counterparts on either side raise their eyebrows as if to endorse the action. They appear to be around my age but they possess a fragility and inexperience which shows on their faces.

Although I smile surreptitiously, I am surprised by their lack of response. The military has succeeded in producing a disciplined, uncaring prototype soldier programmed to kill efficiently both people and emotions — in the same way the Church de-personalises and programmes men's actions and loyalties. A point that I had stressed to my father:

> The Church is a lie if it destroys a person's individuality in order to control his destiny. And God is a lie if men and women can only relate to Him through a Church. Today the Church's mission is more to deceive than to receive humanity unto it. I refuse to be part of this universal fraud which bolsters the immorality of oppression and murder. I write this letter primarily to declare my love for you though, as a child I cannot remember any manifestations of that love — which, sadly, was also lacking in me towards my own son. In that way, I am just as dismal a failure as you are. But despite everything, I still love you deeply.

A powerful icy wind blows into the courtyard and causes the dangling bodies to swing to and fro with hair blowing into their faces — like leaves dancing to the rhythm of an unseen orchestra. The Ice Man jerks the ropes on my wrists as we resume the walk to the scaffold. Somehow I feel pity for his rigidity and show of force. Once during the interminable sessions of interrogation, when we were alone in the cell, he hit me when I refused to reply to his questions. His huge fists cut my lip and I retaliated by hitting him with my head, inflicting a deep gash on his left cheek. Like an enraged animal — which I now realise he is — he savagely assaulted me, his powerful hands locking around my throat. I gasped and remonstrated as his eyes widened and nearly burst with blood. He was sending me to a premature execution but I held on, refusing to submit.

Another guard entered the cell and pulled him away, carrying me with the force of the motion. His grip loosened reluctantly and we fell in opposite directions — each of us stained by the other's blood and hate which now further separates and defines our loyalties. Just as it had been between my father and me.

I was out of the country at the time on a military and diplomatic mission. The coup against our government was swift and terrible, masterminded by several highly-placed civilians including the clergy who had in fact sowed the seeds of the revolt from their pulpits. Many people died and within weeks the usurpers declared a republic in the name of some religion — Christianity, Hinduism, Bhuddism or Islam — call it what you will. On radio and television stations locally and abroad, the usurpers announced:

> We the people of God, justified in the overthrow of the evil and decadent government of the atheists, announce to our nation and the world at large, that we have retrieved the shrines and holy places of our God and have established the rule of religion for all time.

They said nothing about the dead and the maimed, the persecuted and the destitute and those many people who were butchered in the name of their deity. My own father was among them and he had sharpened his ritual blade against the wrongdoers — the atheists and sinners — or so he had warned me in a telephone call from home:

'Son, the people have purged our country of all the atheists, the communists, the liberals and the promiscuous modernists. The drug pedlars and sinful hedonists have been executed. The land is purged and purified.'

'At what price father? So many dead!'

'In God's war, in the war against the ungodly, we do not count the dead. Blood must be shed in order to reclaim and reestablish the kingdom in His name. The government you so loyally serve has been crushed and a true and lasting freedom in the Creator has been set up!'

I disagreed: 'True liberation came when our country fought and gained independence from the imperialists and established a democracy based on the will of the people — not on the military nor the Church. Now it is the rule of the clergy and the state in the name of religion and morality.'

'You must return at once and declare your allegiance to the new state and humble yourself to the divine authority of the holy Church or be destroyed with the enemy. The choice is yours,' said my father.

'When I do return it will be only to fight and overthrow that regime. Do you hear me father, I WILL return!'

He left me hanging on the line just like the two bodies still dangling before me in the wind. Just as I too will soon be dancing — blue or purple in the face with my tongue sticking out. The senior officer is within touching distance of the appointed scaffold. The wind grows stronger and blows off his cap. The three junior sentinels leave their posts to chase bravely after it. Is it the miracle I saw in that vision? Would the wind indeed lift me now with its powerful wings and carry me above the prison walls, across the sea and to freedom? Is this the manifestation of the hurricane I saw in my dream — sweeping madly against the tall steel barricades of a shrine where my father meditated? The building had crumbled on top of him while I rose higher — laughing and shouting hysterically. Could this be it?

The Ice Man retrieves the cap, dusts it off briskly with all the ardour of a loyal soldier and hands it to his peer. Heads nod and I realise that my feet are still firmly on the ground. The vision is buried. The expectation was foolish and I am angry at myself. But Memory is different. It can take you to a time and place beyond torment and pain. Beyond the reach of politics and warfare — where as a child on your mother's lap or playing in the yard or by the orange trees, you feared nothing and no-one.

Memory is stronger than the wind.

As a child I always wanted to be a soldier. My parents proposed the Church or the teaching profession for me their last-born son. My father was fifty years old and my mother forty-six when I was born. I did not fully enjoy their parenthood, and unlike most of the children of our village who played games, I turned to books and developed an above-average intelligence. People spoke about the great things that lay ahead for me and my family. One farmer correctly predicted that I would be hanging — though he referred to my portrait — alongside great and distinguished men and women.

I take another look at the hanging twins, and wonder if they were distinguished achievers. No, they cannot have been. Martyrs are moulded from sterner material, dying with martial anthems on their lips — not with purple or blue tongues protruding from their mouths. None of Shakespeare's tragic characters, including the scandalmongering jester Polonius, was reported to have died with his tongue sticking out. It won't happen to me.

The junior officers ascend the wooden steps. Thirty-three in all, excluding the scaffold platform. They examine the rope and the trapdoor. Satisfied that everything is in executing condition, they salute and stand at attention. Straight and stiff. I turn to face the Ice Man and watch him produce his dirty front teeth. The action is almost indiscernible and I smile for the fun of it — goading him to reveal his suppressed glee of vengeance.

He is disciplined to the teeth and reveals nothing. The senior man blinks and nods at him and the Ice Man grips my wrists and with a nudge of his knee urges me to climb the thirty-three steps.

One.

Two.

Three.

Four.

Five . . . .

When I was five years old my two elder sisters whom I never

really knew nor cared for during my childhood prepared me for my first day at school. At fifty-five my father was a tired man though avidly involved in the affairs of the Church. My mother was sickly and had instructed my sisters to do the work normally done by her. She told me to be quiet and well-behaved — virtues my father had drummed and beaten into me along with rigorous indoctrination in the ways of the spirit. But what I could not fully comprehend or respond to in theology, I found in secular education — winning first grades until the age of twelve. My teachers often visited our home with stories of my intellect and perception, saying that with careful guidance and tuition, I could reach for the stars.

Right now I am reaching the twentieth step and I feel like starting the journey of my life all over again or even from the cell where the sun first greeted and infused me with warmth and courage. I tell myself that I may have skipped two steps or so and I turn round to trace the folly. So much pain has flowed under the bridge of my life. Grim and murky as the end that awaits me. I think of M whose doe-like eyes had flashed at me. Then she was gone and I graduated from university to join the military cadet school to train as a soldier-cum-diplomat. I took my honours in political science and later enlisted in the permanent military force.

The Ice Man coughs and I glance sideways to observe a person in full religious garb enter the courtyard from the narrow door leading from the cells. He is holding what must be a holy book. As he approaches us, I stare at him. Our eyes meet and the second vision reappears as the reel of memory presses on the rewind button. Where, where have I seen his face before? Ah, the man on the hill with the shining book, who rode on the back of a huge bird that lifted me from the depths of a snakepit. But it cannot be, for I have already been rescued once, as one of the demands of a group of hijackers who held more than two hundred passengers hostage after seizing a plane at the local airport.

After two years in exile I returned secretly to the country to spearhead the insurrection. The revolt failed. We had overestimated our chances of victory, having pinned our hopes on the military involvement of a state whose leaders had expressed support for our cause. We were left in the lurch and suffered great losses. Hundreds of our people were killed and arrested. I was wounded and captured alongside many of my comrades. My wife and son were allowed to visit me at the prison hospital — a reunion I will not forget. My son G was afraid of me and ran away crying bitterly. I had failed him as a father. I stared at his mother, refusing to embrace her. I watched her walk away, broken and distraught. She stopped at the swinging doors, turned round to look at me and ran back screaming and calling my name. She embraced me:

'Why me? Why the coldness? I have always loved you. Why hurt me when all I wanted was happiness? To have a home and live with you. Why couldn't I have that life? Why, God, why?'

She was in tears. Her brother, who had captured me, pulled her away and looked deep into my eyes. He hated me and I knew it. I stared at my wife — emptied and dispassionate. Saying nothing, feeling nothing for her.

I was personally disappointed for having led the failed uprising. I knew that history would be cruel to me. The usurpers would guarantee that. I would be sacrificed on the altar of political and religious expediency.

Then came the hijack drama and the demand for my release and safe passage out of the country. As I walked through the prison corridor, I came face-to-cold-face with my brother-in-law. I smiled triumphantly at him but he spat in my face.

'I will get you yet, traitor. You have ruined my sister's life. I shall personally hunt you down wherever you are and bring you back to this scaffold. That rope will always have your name on it. Always.'

His words echo in my mind as the priest instructs the soldiers to remove the bodies of the hanged men. They do not delay and jump at his command. The Church is the state and the state, the Church.

'We promised their families they could have the bodies for burial. We must at all times show compassion and concern towards our citizens. Take them off now.'

I know that he is addressing me and I laugh quietly as he pushes the mischievous tongues back into their rightful domains. The Ice Man looks at me and grins. I get his message and promise myself that I will rather bite off my tongue than have it jutting out of my mouth. The soldiers carry the corpses led by the priest who begins to mumble an incoherent incantation. Once at the tiny door, he turns back and approaches me — his trained sacerdotal eyes reaching into my very being. He must be wondering whether I will seek his forgiveness and atone for my sins at this obviously late, late hour.

Never.

The four hijackers had taken their position inside the aircraft and were heavily armed with an assortment of automatic weapons and grenades. One of them flung a pistol. They were fellow countrymen — young and unknown to me. The tallest and most bearded one addressed me:

'Welcome, comrade. Our demands have been met so far. Release only those women with children and some of the older passengers. The rest are our tickets to freedom. Go!'

The instruction was as cold as the man who gave it. One by one those who qualified for release walked cautiously towards the exit point from the aircraft. I crouched away from the lenses of the military snipers. The captain was ordered to start the engines. My heart beat faster. The iron bird and freedom. Would I ever see my country again? My parents and my little son and a wife I couldn't love? I was escaping from certain death and life waited ahead.

Those had been my thoughts in the aircraft yet now, how

disappointed I am watching the priest. I continue my climb. I notice that his shoes are caked in red mud — obviously from the cemetery. I wonder how many bodies he has personally buried. He has mustered enough courage and I watch him climb the steps. Twenty-three, twenty-four. His words give me no comfort:

'My son, will you not let me pray for you? You are so young. How could you have rejected so much — your beautiful wife, your aged parents and your dear child? Let me pray for you.'

I bite my lip instead and stare fixedly and impassively. I am not going to be prayed over like a kosher offering. I have committed no crime. Neither as a soldier nor as a father. My cause is just no matter what the Church or the state does to me. He appears to be reading my thoughts and replies:

'My son, listen to me. God loves you. Please pray with me!'

His unctuous tone gives me no warmth and I watch him descend the twenty-four steps — a loser. Dejected by my silent rejection of compassion and his god. Nine more steps await me. Nine steps to oblivion. I once read that cowards died many times before they were finally dead. I die with every step I take and I do not think I am a coward. The Ice Man nudges me again as the disappointed priest vanishes from sight. The delay has been unnecessary. Time to go.

Step number twenty-five. The year of my decoration for valour in the face of the enemy. The military parade. The march to the rostrum and the decoration. Then my engagement to G's mother and a master's degree at twenty-eight.

Twenty-nine steps climbed. Four more to go.

While we waited for the aircraft to take off, one of the male passengers dashed past me as the last woman and her child alighted. I saw him roll down the steps and run to one side. The order came:

'Shoot dammit, shoot!'

I could not. I was not at war with him nor with any of the other passengers. They were tickets to freedom.

'I can't shoot!'

I heard a shot.

I watched him run.

I saw him fall.

We are now at step number thirty. The vision of my marriage shoots past like a meteor — as did our brief sexual consummation. A few drops of blood. The unfulfilled wedding bliss — all seemed to be overshadowed by the odour of oranges in the orchard where M and I had sought and found each other. Full and ripe and ready — scanning and searching the heights together. Then I was lifted high, a phoenix from the flames of passion. Strong, and a man. But where is she, where is my M?

The ropes move in the wind, whipping wildly like a weak branch. Gone are the days when people were hanged from trees. Thirty-two steps. Are my sisters and my mother awake? Is she praying for me? Will the usurpers allow her to bury me? Where will the grave be? Under the orange trees or by the foot of the hill near the village where I was born — and where my father is buried?

Death is long.

Then they stormed the aircraft. Blood and bodies, as thousands of bullets sprayed the interior. So many dead including my rescuers — blasted before my very eyes. Men and women screaming, weeping. A bullet ripped through my arm, another pierced my leg. I was recaptured, hospitalised and humiliated all over again. My brother-in-law had led the invasion. I no longer believe in visions. I decide this as the guard grabs the dancing noose and I feel the Ice Man push me to move on. Will I meet him perchance in that country 'from whose bourne no traveller returns'? It is the final step — step number thirty-three. If there is a place called hell, will I meet my father there? What will we say to each other — if talking were allowed in that place?

My father, the patriot. The usurpers honoured him for having exposed me as the chief plotter and insurrectionist following our abortive telephone discussion during my exile. I vowed to return to help overthrow the regime. No greater love hath a man than this, that he lays down the life and honour of his son for the Church and the state. They decorated him, but two days later he died. The passionate prison letter to him in which I questioned the existence of God, was produced by the state as proof of my heretical and atheistic crimes against the Church. It was a trial in which I refused to plead or take their oath:

'I do not recognise the validity nor power of this circus nor of those butchers who sit in judgment over me. They are the real traitors. This regime and its hypocritical Church, and those scheming priests who preach meekness to the people and grow fat and rich on suffering, should be on trial here! I refuse to be judged by butchers.'

My words brought a tense silence to the courtroom. I heard someone's knuckles crack like soft machinegun fire against my ears. A lone woman jumped to her feet and raised her gloved right hand as the courtroom fan blew into her face and flung her hair to the back of her head. She screamed:

'Priests, butchers, clowns and traitors — murdering and ruling in the name of the law and of the Church! You are not alone, comrade and you will not die in vain!'

They dragged her out still shouting. I felt encouraged but sad that my utterings — like the failed revolt and the hijack failure — had given the usurpers yet another victim. Could she perhaps have been my M? Establishing my guilt was a mere formality, as were my conviction and the imposition of the seven death sentences. The circus was packed to capacity. All the tickets were sold out. Two weeks of clowns and animals came to a close. It was feeding time. The lions and tigers of the law and the Church had to be fed. The lamb of insurrection and sedition would be slaughtered, and its blood be given up, as my father had always reminded me during my youth. This was the law. The foundation and touchstone upon which all the decadent morality of the state and the Church had been built. From Adam to Abraham, Jacob to Joseph, and from Moses right down the long line to Jesus.

The law.

The life.

Guilty as charged.

I examined the judge's eyes. I marvelled at the hairy hand that held up his beaming and golden face — to be admired and feared. Yes, it comes to me now, that third vision. That massive wheel which had imprints of my head on both sides. Spinning fast and rolling into the streets — down and away from the crowds. My life was a coin in the judge's fingers. Heads I die. Tails I die.

Now I take my final look at the sky. The sun, my brief ally, hides behind dark, voluptuous clouds which hang low over the rooftops like grey breasts dripping their milk of despair on to the stark prison. I cough deep-throated and swallow my spit. I feel it slide reluctantly down my gullet. My feet are mortuary cold and the blood on both my big toes has dried. The lower parts of my body become mysteriously anaesthetised — dying before their time, and chickening out on the top half. I want to collapse but warm trickles of urine against my left thigh restore the electrical short-circuit and I hold on.

One moment, one billion moments have flashed through my mind since that sixteenth step at my prison cell. I think of the two hanged trailblazers who have gone ahead. I gaze inquisitively at the junior officers in the hope that I will detect a softening of their stiff stares. I marvel also at the cold precision with which they perform, no, execute their duties, but nothing is revealed. I see the faces of my mother and my sisters and the woman called M. They shatter into a million fragments. The mother of my son appears briefly before the lens of the mental camera. There is a click and she too recedes into the twilight mist. A face without a name. I too have no name. I am every man. I live everywhere. I die every day.

My thoughts are for my son. Will his embittered mother — hurt as she is and may well be for the rest of her life — speak kindly of me? Will she give him those medallions and my watch — the final tokens of my love for him? Will she? What we don't know cannot hurt us. Whoever said that was lying. I feel a deep, gripping pain inside my being. I want to cry, dammit. If only I could see him just one more time. Just to hold him and feel his breath on my lips. I must hold on. I must not let the enemy observe this moment of weakness.

I have read and heard and known of people who have continued to live long after they died. Men and women whose names have been carved on the rocks of struggle and human sacrifice and etched on the memory of their people. The children sing of them. Women ululate their names from the mountaintops and the valleys to the stone and granite cities of the world. Alive. Cherished. Loved. I have heard and read and known of people who continue to live beyond their graves. Will it be the same for me? Will someone remember my face?

The noose has been thoughtfully rolled with calico to avoid or minimise bruising and discomfort. The senior officer places it over my head and I feel it soft against my neck. A coldness envelopes me. I am afraid. I want to scream. I want to call out for help. My body shakes uncontrollably. I don't want to die. God, I don't want to die. The senior officer tightens the rope — pulling it firmly yet without malice. Our eyes meet. Deep and full. I make myself believe that he sees the hidden anguish and fear that tug at my heart. I read his life on the pockmarks and trace his youth in the village. In my mind's eye, I see him playing soldier just as I once did. The executioner and the victim are one. Our eyes widen once more — waiting for the final acknowledgement. He blinks twice. Slow and full of empathy — opening and closing both eyes. He locks his stern jaws and looks away. The compassion I receive from the act warms me and pacifies my fear. The coldness vanishes. My strength is renewed and increased. I respond and pull the sides of my mouth into a grin at first, and then into a full, beaming smile. Strong and ready for the unknown.

The golden seagull soars in my mind — its pinions firmly poised as it prepares to plunge into the sea.

The trapdoor gives way.

I feel the weight of my body sink rapidly, stretching my neck. Sinking and falling into a deep, deep gorge. Several vertebrae crack like knuckles. The taste and odour of oranges invade my senses. M's eyes smile at me. Clear and brown.

Darkness . . . .

OGGZEE

You just could not look at Oggzee once. His was the kind of face that demanded, and received, second or third glances. It had nothing to do with beauty or handsomeness or the absence of either for that matter. The man was simply attractive — as a powerful magnet draws all sorts of objects to it, so too did Oggzee's face turn heads wherever he went. He gave Helen of Troy a veritable facial run for her money. Wherever he showed his countenance, our man launched thousands of stares and just as many grins and bursts of laughter.

'Grass does not grow out of a rock', was Oggzee's jocular but abrupt dismissal to the countless and persistent queries about the scarcity of hair on his small head. Deep and multiple furrows in parallel formation cut across his protruding brow which always glistened with natural oil. Oggzee's large eyes appeared to be falling out of their sockets.

I recall with glee how we teased — gwaraa — him when the 3-D movie craze hit Sophiatown in the 1950s. Cinema patrons were sold special spectacles with which to watch the films. But Oggzee never ever bought them.

'Your eyes are 10-D, Oggzee; they can see the whole film blindfolded', a gwaraa-outie teased. In Kofifi-taal this would read: 'Ek sê Oggzee, djou 10-Down glopes ruk chandies sonder sweet; omtesê djy goggle die hele stuk haa sal norch.'

Oggzee's retort: 'These are not ordinary glopes kakjas (shit-coat). I can look at your airzees (arse) and hear your kak scream: "Please help me I'm falling". All I have to do is lift your airzees, count the cobwebs and tell you when you had your last meal.' Oggzee would reply to peals of laughter.

He also had exceptionally wide nostrils which some gwaraa-outies said were boreholes or corridors or tunnels leading to his tiny brain.

'No wonder you can't keep secrets, Oggzee; with such huge tunnels people can easily look inside your nose and actually see what you are thinking.'

Oggzee would good-naturedly split his sides with laughter, but he was always able to come up with a caustic retort which saw some of the gwaraa-outies being reduced to 'gwaraa-moegoes'.

'Ja, remember the time you were so thirsty and you opened your mouth under my nose. You nearly drowned in my snot, bright boy!' Our hero would then press his long thumb, with its uncut nail, hard against his nostril. The eruption would either land into the sand or on to the teaser's foot or shoe. Those of us who were accustomed to this form of 'haal' jibe always got our money's worth. Some of the moegoes just vomited. Yhegg!

That was Oggzee.

And the fact that his nostrils rested comfortably on one of his large lips also earned him the name of Mouth. But that was by no means his only name. He went by several others: Ntibidi; Ndibilishi; Oogies (eyes); Dinko (nose); Ou Tata (old man) and Molausi which turned out to be his surname. He lived, and in a way relished, his many names. They added to his gregariousness and extrovert personality. He sang at weddings and at funeral wakes and became a hot favourite among the girls. One of them bore his three children but vanished soon after the removals of Sophiatown. Oggzee was a film fundi and could recite lines from Laurence Olivier's *Hamlet* which we saw several times over at the Odin Bioscope where he and I had worked — at different times — as poorly-paid ushers. He knew the names of acts by heart, and young kids sometimes paid him two pennies to listen to his ghost stories and folk-tales.

'Kakprater' — howler — was one of many names he acquired on account of his ability to relate anecdotes — mostly tall stories, and jokes of the side-splitting variety, which had most of the guys rolling in the mud and slime of Kofifi-Sophia. Such was the oral mastery of Oggzee, the man with many names.

He was older than all the chaps in our gwaraa circle. Jabulani Khubeka, nicknamed 'Pirate' (now dead), who had a deep and shiny ebony complexion which earned him the name 'Mnyamane' — the Black One — teased Oggzee about his age.

'Your folks were so poor all they left you was old age!' We rocked with laughter.

'Hey, wena Mnyamane,' retorted Oggzee, 'you are so black that when Muhle (the Native Affairs Commissioner) asked for your birth certificate, you brought a wheelbarrow full of coal.'

That took care of Pirate.

If ever there were two bosom kakpraters it was Oggzee and me. Some guys even teased us, naming us after two American comic-book wisecrackers, Mutt and Jeff. We were considered to be among the wittiest gwaraa kings in the kakpraat business in the ghettos of Kofifi, Die Kaas (Western Native Township) and Maglera or Chinatown and Sidikidiki or Annakant-Die-Spoor — the names that the people gave to Newclare, a freehold township opposite Die Kaas that stretched westward towards the poor white township of Claremont, where the underpaid railway Boers resided. In the true tradition of the Western: the big showdown to see who was the fastest kakprater alive, the various territorial gwaraa-outies challenged one another. The showdown venue was the football field in Die Kaas at an already dug-out trench which led rainwater into a sewerage tunnel that only the daring had ventured to enter. 'Die Tonolie' as it was called, had its mouth at the very end of Maglera at Makouvlei — better known in the old Sophiatown days as Matikitwan — the open area where black people scavenged the huge refuse heaps where the Johannesburg City Council dumped the trash that came from the rich white areas. Big stores like *John Orrs,*

Greatermans and *The Belfast* also dumped their reject goods at Matikitwan.

The various supporting factions always sat on opposite sides to laugh and cajole and whistle at the kak-wieties and the haalle we flung at each other. Pirate, another gwaraa chief, played the role of referee. Fights often broke out across the trenches when some of the haalle became too personal or too caustic. One never touched on someone's mother. To gwaraa a father or any male relative or even a granny, was permitted in some cases. But touch on an ou-lady or a mamtana or a ma-griezen and the blood would flow. That was really asking for trouble. But no-one ever fought Oggzee. He was a peaceable man who never touched anyone's mother no matter the provocation. Perhaps it was because he never experienced the joy and comfort of living with his own mother, or so we guessed.

There were many adults and older boys and girls who frequented the gwaraa-stiefies at the football field. 'Stiefie' — derived from stiff, was the word we gave to clean fist fights between two or more streetfighters who bashed each other without the use of knives or other lethal weapons. 'Haai bamba, haai luma' (no holding, no biting) was the commonly-used phrase to describe these stiefies.

But Oggzee out-gwaraa-ed everyone including me. He was the king; the most loved and respected mouth and the Number One kakprater in Kofifi, or so we all believed.

In 1953, Oggzee and I applied for membership of the popular African Morning Stars Football Club established in Sophia-town in 1927. The meeting was held at a dingy one-room dwelling on the corner of Edward Road and Ray Street, known at the time as 'Berlin Territory' — the domain of the ruthless and notorious Berliners Gang who ruled Edward Road and the whole northern section of Sophiatown. The venue was diagonally opposite the Princess Alice Hospital situated at the bottom of the Christ the King Anglican Church in Ray Street.

Skeins of smoke from pipes and cigarettes curled towards the off-white ceiling and hung defiantly over the heads of the football club members. The room was overcrowded and humid. About fifty long-standing as well as newly-recruited players stood around or leaned against the zinc and plank fencing in the yard. A tall, pipe-smoking man with a clean-shaven head, who wore an expensive tweed suit, introduced himself as Makgato. He was the club's chairman or the 'Pressa' — the colloquial name given to the president of a sports club — and a term still widely used today in amateur football circles in the black townships. Pressas were the ones who spent their money on the club, made the rules and guided the club's destiny. They were a venerated bunch and were held in very high esteem. Makgato, who died after the Sophiatown removals, was one such a man.

When the time came for the registration of new members, Oggzee was the first to jump to his small feet and thin legs. The dialogue was in Kofifi-taal. In fact, everyday communication was conducted in the Taal. Oggzee was known to many of the people present.

'Hoe roep ons djou, outie?' (What's your name, fellow?)

'Aah, ek het geeleek name!' (I've many names!)

'Chee aa een; roep outie.' (Give one; speak fellow.)

Oggzee's eyes lit up and swelled like a balloon inflated by a hidden diabolical breeze. He smiled impishly and opened his mouth so widely one could see many empty spaces in his gums. He searched the Pressa's face and scanned the eyes of the other members, including the club secretary Steve 'Twa-Twa' Rathebe who appeared to be puzzled by Oggzee's behaviour.

We all waited anxiously. But the eventual response was well worth waiting for.

'Ek es ou Stanley Mechooz,' declared Oggzee.

The dingy room shook with uncontrollable laughter. For more than three minutes everyone in the house and in the yard laughed until tears streamed down their cheeks. The pronunciation of the British football star's name was the cause for the hilarity.

'Stanley Mechooz? Stanley Mechooz, my gat' (arse), shouted Makgato and puffed hard at his pipe. Then amid coughing and fits of laughter, the Pressa said: 'Shit and Bricks! Shit and bloody Bricks es djou kaartjie outie!' Laughter.

And our man Oggzee got himself another name which was to become a rallying call during the entertaining but volatile football matches. He also refused to disclose his age, saying that it was between him and his parents.

'Helle es saat, zaaltee,' an irritated Oggzee said in the Taal.

'Saat' and 'zaaltee' were synonyms for 'deceased'. That was the lingo that the people 'cabled' and one which Oggzee had helped to enrich with his own contrived colloquialisms. 'Hintee', 'tolayzen' and 'nyaatat' were other such synonyms including the phrase: 'Hy's sand gonees toe' — gone to the sand blanket; the cemetery. Although Oggzee was a Taal innovator, he was no tsotsi. The Casbah — a gang haunt of the Victoria Street's Casbah Kids — was one of his many 'blom-plekke', haunts, but he moved around freely. He was a regular at the football field in Western Native Township across Sophiatown which was divided by tramlines and the famous Main Road.

No-one knew Oggzee's origins nor who his parents were. His only known kin was a younger brother Baans or Banthatha whose huge nostrils — much larger than Oggzee's, also earned him the name of 'Dinko'. They were both chronic gamblers, conmen and big eaters, and extremely dedicated to one another. Baans died in Oggzee's arms. He was hit by a car. It was a most heart-rending experience to see our gwaraa hero sob bitterly in the middle of Good Street. Oggzee hit his head hard against the concrete pavement until he bled. He called for his mother. 'Gootee' (Good Street) stood still that day. Oggzee was loved and respected by many and we all shared his grief and loss including children who worshipped him because of his ability to make them laugh.

Our hero hated the abominable pass or dompas as the rural folk from Transkei dubbed the so-called Reference Book. He refused to obtain one and would dodge the pass raiders at every opportunity. The 'Sament Baaikies' (cement coats), the name Oggzee gave to the police because of their stiffly-buttoned uniforms, could never catch him during their frequent raids. He out-ran and out-thought them and made fools of them at every turn. When new recruits came to Sophiatown to learn the tricks of their hated trade, Oggzee would taunt them.

One day, a short and stocky Boer 'gataa' and his squad of 'native' constables, cornered us at a dice game in a narrow, cramped alley. We jumped the wall and dashed into Western. We saw Oggzee coming up the Main Road pavement that led to Balanski, the cheap, bug-infested cinema just off Bertha Street. Disappointed at not having caught us, the police stopped people and demanded to see their passes. There were some arrests.

As the Boer approached our man, an instantaneous and remarkable transformation occurred: Oggzee became a handicapped person. The fingers on his left hand shrunk, his mouth twisted to one side and his left leg contracted as the heel rose from the ground. It was a marvel to behold as he hobbled clumsily like a drunk while his head shook like a reed in the wind. The Boer stopped, scrutinised our hero from head to toe and then allowed him to pass unhindered. It had never happened before and we whistled and cheered our gwaraa king who, after having fooled the gataa sauntered towards the door of the Balanski. Thinking that Oggzee was a genuine cripple, 'Die Jood' — the Jewish owner — allowed him to enter the cinema free of charge. After that incident handicapped people never paid at Balanski, and for that we respected Die Jood.

When a squad of pass raiders swooped on the same area, Oggzee repeated the hoax but one of the darkie gataas was not easily convinced: 'Hey baba, yesterday you were cripple on the left side, now today it's on the right hand side; listen, I'm no fokken fool!'

'Gaamph, gaamph,' splattered the saliva-dripping conman in disagreement, 'that waasch my small braadaa; not me, stroessch God.'

The policeman shook his head in open amazement. He pushed Oggzee aside. 'Fok off man, go!' Our hero hobbled past, his almost bald head shaking pitiably.

A few days later Oggzee underwent a severe transformation — he became a double cripple.

Well, it happened this way.

We were jiving and jitterbugging at the corner of Gootee and Main Road on the pavement outside Chait's Jewish Butchery and Saloojee's Music Saloon and Cycle Works. Some of us were out of breath and we watched Oggzee take on a few 'charo-wiebiets' — girls — to the beat of Louis Jordan's 'Pine Tops Boogie Woogie'. Our hero's tongue hung over his lower lip while his right index finger pointed in the air as he shook his lithe five-foot frame. He was in a world of his own as his knees moved in and out like those of the legendary American blues singer and dancer Cab Calloway.

Someone shouted: 'Araraai! chandies ruk; stinka gataas, majieta!'

That was all that was needed for the double transformation. The pass raiders — and to crown it all the same Boer who had had the initial 'cripple' encounter with Oggzee — crossed the road and advanced on us. It was too late; our hero could not run. Instead his delicate hands shrunk. His knees buckled and became jelly. He sagged and twisted his body. Our super contortionist frothed at the mouth. He spat and slurred badly. His heels rose steadily as if jacked up by an invisible contraption. He did one of the fanciest tiptoe jigs ever witnessed at the busy and populated corner. By that time most of the other guys had scattered to safety.

I was a so-called coloured — 'aa bushie' — and was therefore not obliged by law to possess the hated stinka, so I stood around.

'Paaas! Paaas!' The Boer dragged the word as he approached. His voice, like his belted hip, carried the mark of a power firmly entrenched in the holster and in the uniform which he wore. The power that came with being a law enforcer. It had everything to do with pigmentation, and yet paradoxically, nothing to do with it. In the former, it related to and was exemplified in the colour and conduct of the Boer (who represented the white man's law) against the African people. And latterly, the contention of colour was summarily waived when black and white wore the same uniform and represented the same law — although in the same breath black policemen were forced by the same law to carry a dompas.

'Hey cripple-gat,' said the Boer. 'I saw you the other day and you were cripple on your bleddie left side!' He had a good memory; one could see in his eyes that he was no fool. He blared again: 'Ja, one of my native boys says he saw someone like you who was cripple on the right hand side. What the hell's going on eh?'

Oggzee was caught off-guard by the Boer's sharp words.

'Yessch, my baasch,' spluttered our hero. 'Helle waasch altwee my braadaasch!' The saliva of a sly trickster rolled down the sides of his big mouth.

'Fok!' exclaimed the Boer. 'Cripple-gat of nie cripple-gat nie, kom fokken saam!' As Oggzee was being dragged towards the kwela-kwela he rapidly wriggled, twisted his body and shot out of his persecutor's grip. He adroitly dashed across Main Road and passed through the iron railings into Die Kaas. The baffled Boer scratched his head and laughed heartily: 'Gott daai cripple-gat kan hardloop!' he said.

That was the kind of guy Oggzee was.

He defiantly refused to carry a stinka. He did not have regular employment and undertook odd jobs when the opportunity availed itself. And that was not often. Our hero did not possess a house nor did he ever pay the poll and personal taxation which was compulsory for all African adults.

'I'll never give a penny to Baas Sampie,' Oggzee told us when questioned about his refusal to pay the poll tax. 'Baas Sampie' was Oggzee's South African counterpart of America's Uncle Sam.

Oggzee's continuing rebelliousness against the pass system induced many young people to oppose its imposition although the time would come when its possession would be vital in the procurement of jobs and accommodation. But until that came, pass dodging would be the order of the day. Many emulated him because he was the epitome of an inexhaustible ingenuity and cunning.

During and after the Second World War many African people, particularly the war veterans, were granted special Exemption Certificates by the government of General Smuts which allowed for free mobility, and an exemption against the forced possession of the pass. But the 1948 election victory by the Afrikaner Nationalists nullified that and many other Smuts concessions, and accelerated the arbitrary imposition of the pass and influx laws that turned many Africans into criminals when they 'failed to produce' — to use the fashionable term of that day.

Oggzee was one of many people who contrived ruses to escape the daily pass harassment and dragnets by squads of over-zealous policemen. Our hero manufactured his own 'Zamshin Sertifikate Pass' by pasting together two broadsheets of newspaper or the standard white wrapping paper used by butchers. When fully opened, and after several neat folds, appeared the words: 'Zamshin Sertifikate Pass — General Smuts.'

All in Oggzee's very own spelling.

Our gwaraa king folded his 'identity document' until it fitted neatly into his back trousers pocket — the traditional domain and habitat of all pass books and assault knives like the feared Three Button alias 'The Three Star' and the Bozaalino knife with its distinctive thick blade.

For the cheek of it Oggzee secured his invention with a broad piece of elastic band. He produced many such Zamshins most of which were for personal use, while some were offered for sale. And they never failed to work — unless of course they were tried on the same pass persecutor more than once.

Picture our hero strolling unperturbed and bravely towards the waiting arms of an advancing 'darkie' or Boer gataa who would normally prefer the traditional noisy pursuit through the streets and alleys. Not only were the Law's arms strong, they could also punch hard; and its boots rob one of breath. But that time there was no running nor the echo of the police-whistle; just a loud: 'Paaas jong!'

'I don't wear a pass.'

'What? You don't wear a pass? Who do you think you are — King George?'

'Naa. I'm a General Smuts ex-souljaa. I wear a Zamshin Sertifikate Pass — General Smuts.'

'Smuts; Smuts se moer. Lemme see that Zamshin kak of yours.'

Obeying with a note of smug impudence, almost as if to impugn the authority of his persecutor, Oggzee would firstly rummage through his pockets. The next command would blare against the eardrum: 'Kom aan jong; roer jou fokken gat.'

Finally acquiescing to the 'shake your arse' command our hero would hand over his Zamshin.

'What the fokken hell is this thing?'

'My Zamshin.'

'Your Zamshin, BAAS!' (In the case of a Boer policeman.)

'My Zamshin, BAAS.'

A stream of the usual torrent of saliva would fly at the baas. After wiping his face and cursing or even throwing the instinctive punch, the Boer would remove the elastic band in full view of many inquisitive onlookers. Our hero's eyes glowed with the traditional impishness of a delinquent schoolboy.

When Fold Number One was accomplished, the pass raider would grapple with the others. When the arms were fully outstretched, the words 'Zamshin Sertifikate Pass — General Smuts' would jump at him.

'What the hell is this kak?' the bewildered and angry raider would demand, and on throwing the broadsheet aside either to hit or grab his quarry, the Boer would gape in amazement at the spot where Oggzee was. Oggzee, who had scurried to safety at the fifth or sixth fold, would be seen leaning against the iron railings across the Main Road, casually picking the few teeth in his grinning mouth.

And the amused onlookers, particularly those close to the baas, would cautiously wait for the cue: if the baas scratched his German-cut head and laughed in pleasant wrath and perplexity, they too would join in. Otherwise silence was safety; was preservation. When the baas was out of sight and far, very far from arm's length, their reverberating laughter would become a form of applause for our ingenious hero.

That was Oggzee.

During the winter of 1954, amid escapades of streetfighting and of being wounded and jailed, I was selected to play alongside Oggzee in a second division cup final game. Our opponents, Aberleen Home Boys' were tough no-nonsense Orlando East-based footballers. They were rowdy, stick-wielding Zulu tribesmen who lived in the hostels. They were one team no-one easily challenged to a fight.

We were down one-nil.

The match, played at the Wemmer Sports Ground — at what is now a Johannesburg City Council parking lot in Loveday Street — attracted a huge, noisy crowd. But to no avail. All appeared lost. In the dying minutes of the match, and after a lot of rough play and cuts and bruises, we were awarded a corner kick. As the ball soared towards the Aberleen goalposts, their bearded and continuously growling goalkeeper, shot up to collect the ball, his arms reaching high above our heads. Oggzee who had apparently hidden behind the white line, pulled the goalkeeper's pants and underwear down to his knees. The shocked man's private parts and his backside caught the cool winter breeze.

'My balas! My airzees!' screamed the bewildered man as he covered himself with his hands. The ball rested at the back of the net. The referee, who swore by his mother he had not seen anything, awarded the much-needed draw goal. All hell broke loose. The stick-wielding supporters and the Aberleen players attacked all and sundry, including the referee. They inflicted deep gashes and ugly bruises on the heads of many. We fled across the field. I bled from a cut on my head but a voice inside told me to run, boy, run. And run we did, right into the heart of the Golden City. Bloodied but laughing.

Oggzee was nowhere in sight. We feared the worst. When we finally arrived at our favourite haunt in Good Street, we found our gwaraa leader at Foi Chew's Trading Store. He pushed a handful of roasted peanuts into his mouth and chewed as if nothing had happened. Foi Chew, the four-foot Chinese motor mechanic, sold the tastiest 'knakkers' in all Kofifi. We had learned — or rather Oggzee had trained us — never to dare ask him for peanuts. And if someone did, our hero would stuff his mouth full, and amid furious chewing with saliva streaming down the sides of his lips, he would say: 'Gaan knak djou aigene knakkers, moegoe.' (Get your own nuts, greenhorn.)

His only response to the pants-down incident at the Wemmer football field, was a curt: 'What the hell are you guys crying about? At least we managed to draw . . . .'

That was Oggzee.

When Oggzee Molausi's backyard shack was demolished in

1958 during the final stages of the removal assault on Sophiatown he had never, to my knowledge, had a fight with anyone. He moved to Soweto's Rockville township in the company of thousands of other forcibly ejected African families. We still met frequently at the African Morning Stars' football club matches in Meadowlands and Rockville. Life changed dramatically.

The Sharpeville Massacre came, passed. Poqo of the Pan African Congress made headlines with the attacks at the Bashee River in the Eastern Cape. In December of 1961, the military wing of the African National Congress, Umkhonto we Sizwe, declared its armed offensive against the Apartheid regime, and later, very much later, thousands of Africans were finally resettled in the Meadowlands and Diepkloof townships.

Oggzee was brutally assaulted and stabbed several times. The attack occurred at a shebeen in White City Jabavu not far from the home of his adopted family. Rumour had it that one of the new ilk of 'Makwaaitos' — the Vicious Ones — who ruled that part of the sprawling ghetto, had found our hero's gwaraawieties to be in bad taste. But Oggzee did not die. The knife had done greater damage to his reputation: it penetrated his throat and severed his vocal cords.

He was taken to Coronation Hospital. Pirate and I stood near the bed of our distraught, physically weak and speechless hero. I touched his thin arm. He looked up at us and smiled. The huge eyes were sunken and empty. A week later specialists fitted a gadget into his throat which he could use when there was a need to communicate or remove when he didn't need to. And when Oggzee did speak, it was a far cry from the sharp wit and caustic haalle that had once brought joy and fun to so many people in Kofifi.

The incorrigible Pirate would not let the opportunity pass. Without malice he observed: 'Herre Oggzee, die laanies het aa dek parraa en djou gorrel engaset. Eleke nou-en-dan as daai parraa bodla, dan speel djy djou trumpet!'

Our hero put the gadget into the hole in his throat and

croaked happily until he coughed. Tears glistened on his cheeks. We did not know whether it was because of sadness or joy. Pirate's jibe about a wind-breaking bullfrog in Oggzee's gullet made us laugh with the free abandon and mirth which came only with true and tolerant friendship and camaraderie.

At the time of writing this anecdote about the 'Man with many names', Oggzee still resides with his adopted kin although he has been reported missing or dead on several occasions. Our hero has aged terribly, is haggard and drinks a lot more than he did in the old days. The gadget comes up to his throat now and then whenever he tries to recapture the past when he was the centre of attraction; the kakpraat and gwaraa king — 'aa outie tussen die outies; aa really real majieta en die laaitie van die stuk van kwaai haalle en sharp wieties'.

That was before the bulldozers came.

But the kakpraat and gwaraa legacy lives on whenever people get together to laugh and speak about the old days. And about a man called Oggzee.

THE UNIFORM

1985.

The security key slid silently into the safety lock. It turned thrice until it clicked. One had to be extra careful these days, especially with the escalation of violence and terrorism. The Volk was not only divided unto itself but it faced dark and grim days. The rightwing wolves needed close watching. Although much of what they complain and agitate about is true, they should not allow the Afrikaner to be destroyed. Times were changing and the old ways could not be fully relived.

Majoor Dries Swanepoel rested his head against the door. He was not for division and bickering. The Volk came first and it had to be protected from all kinds of subversion. The Honourable Minister had said so during the Police passing out parade in Pretoria. What he said was true for his words were close to the heart and nerve of this uniform. And did not the Honourable Minister himself declare that patriotism was the very essence and touchstone of Afrikaner survival? And was not the blood and the covenant of the early Boer pioneers etched on human sacrifice against hostile Brit and Bantu?

'Yes, my people,' the Honourable Minister had said, 'we must not let anything — whether far right or invisible left, black or white — stand between the sanctity of your uniform and your commitment to your Volk. Not anything. Not now, not ever!'

Those words had sparked a flame in Dries Swanepoel's soul at the time. The Honourable Minister was correct: not anything, not now: not ever. His huge, hairy hand covered the bronze doorknob and turned it slowly. The grip carried the weight and stamp of the authority of a much-decorated police hero 'whose courage in the face of the enemy during operations in the black townships of South Africa,' as his many citations read, had earned Dries recognition and rapid promotion. He had seen a lot of action and had come out unscathed — or so everyone appeared to believe. Where, where did it all begin?

March 19, 1960

The incidents surrounding that date came alive, particularly that first indoctrination session inside the Sharpeville municipal offices.

'The battle in the native areas of this our Vaderland is not a case of civil war as those liberal communists and their newspapers want the world to believe. Ours is a just and righteous battle against a heathen enemy that seeks to overthrow and destroy all that our Volk and forefathers worked, sacrificed and died for....'

The recruits had listened straight-faced and impassionately. No-one even twitched an eye. If the kommandant said so then that *was* the truth. For truth was in the eye of the beholder. In that instance it wore a police uniform and was armed, ready and willing. That kind of truth was and still is unquestionable, and would be so in years to come, or so the kommandant told himself as he looked into the cold eyes of his young and inexperienced charges.

'But kommandant,' the seventeen-year-old recruit had interjected. 'Are the natives not of this land and a part of the nation? Native or Volk, is this not the common earth of every Suid-Afrikaner?'

All the short-haired German-cut heads turned to look at the Doubting Thomas in their ranks. Dries Swanepoel shuddered as he recalled the cold shivers that ran down his neck at the time.

'Wrong konstabel, wrong. The enemy is that one which seeks and acts out its desire to destroy the very essence and ethos that nourished and sustained our Volk during the early trials of political and religious persecution; oppression and genocide. Such an enemy — be he Native or Brit or Jood — will never truly be a part of this nation. When people fight against your uniform they stand in direct opposition to our law, our Kerk and against our culture. You may be too young to understand these things, Swanepoel, but in time you will; you will . . .'

That was the last word. No-one, let alone a young Boer, had the right to question the Volk. The uniform was what defined friend from foe. The uniform was what made a boy become a man. Finish and klaar! Dries never asked any questions after that incident. In fact he became a model of patriotic soldiery, full of heat and zeal for land and Volk. His careless assumption about a common nationality with Natives was made two days before the Sharpeville Massacre.

Gott, what a bloody mess *that* was, thought Dries. The marchers and the singing descended like a thick, black cloud on to the municipal offices. Gott, what a bloody mess that was.

Most of the Natives held their passes above their heads. They were angry and determined and it was Dries Swanepoel's first encounter with an unrest situation; and one which was to brand itself deep into the very heart and soul of his memory: terrifying yet exciting. The faces of his armed colleagues were stiff and unsmiling and he chose to be like them.

'Take your stinking passes! We Africans are tired of being made slaves and strangers in our own land! Away with the passes! Away!'

The crowd echoed his cry.

Dries aimed his 303 rifle at the speaker's chest. The man in his sights wiped the froth of anger from the sides of his mouth.

Then came the order from the kommandant: 'This is an illegal gathering in terms of the Riotous Assemblies Act. You have exactly three minutes in which to disperse after which we shall be forced to use force.'

The singing stopped. A huge dark cloud blotted the sun above Dries Swanepoel's head. The man in his sights laughed sarcastically.

But these are our people, kommandant.

The young man who had not so long ago uttered those doubtful words, pressed his right forefinger on the trigger. The muscles in his jaws contracted. His teeth sank into his bottom lip. His eyes narrowed. All the energy and the blood and confusion of his seventeen years on earth, were aimed at the tall marcher with the small mouth.

But these are our people.

Wrong konstabel, wrong.

A woman began to sing. Her song was taken up again; loud and strong against Dries Swanepoel's thumping eardrums. Like angry heartbeats. The sound of ululating hit against the darkening sky. Rain and blood were imminent, thought Dries. The marchers in front flung their passes away and turned round to melt into a huge portion of the crowd at the back that had already begun to disperse.

Wrong konstabel, wrong.

There was no command to shoot but Dries remembered firing the first shot. Hundreds more such shots followed over the years: in 1973 at the Carletonville Mines; 1976 and 1977 at Soweto and Alexandra Township where the darkness had made it easy. Then in 1980 at Elsies River and Guguletu; Sebokeng and Sharpeville revisited in 1984 during the great siege. Gott, what bloody messes they all were: stones and dustbin lids against modern fire-power. Will these bloody blacks never learn?

1985.

After the grim carnage: truckloads of Coke and buns and chocolate bars were distributed among the township children, and the football matches that followed with two military vehicles on either side to serve as goalposts.

Gott, we are fokken clever. Shoot and kill them and then offer them cooldrinks and chocolate. Fokken clever, thought Dries as the heavy hand-carved stinkwood door opened quietly. He lowered his seven-foot body so as not to knock his head against the door-frame. It was an instinctive action and he tiptoed into the dimly-lit hallway of his four-bedroomed house. The pinewood floor with its rich odour of polish, creaked at the usual spot. He was not one to wake his Liefie and their two small daughters unnecessarily. In a way he always felt secure inside when the floor creaked. It was a sort of fraternal home-coming to a place and a family he loved and worshipped very deeply. A family which was also blessed with the gentleness and caring of a loving and dedicated father.

Dries Swanepoel's first marriage had ended abruptly. Katrina, the tall, blonde-haired eldest daughter of Dominee Lukas Lodewyk, was said to have flirted with her husband's colleagues during his late night-duty rounds. People whispered dirty rumours about his Katrina whom he had wed and taken as a virgin. He had refused to believe the stories. What could have gone wrong? She was so beautiful. How she had nagged him to leave the police force. He recalled the last heated and almost blasphemous argument before she left. It was over the sanctity of his uniform; no the sanctity of the Volk's uniform.

Right konstabel, right.

'Andries I'm fed up with being the silent and persevering wife of a policeman; living in patient poverty while the wives of other men dress up and eat better. Sick of your constant reminders of duty to that damned uniform!'

'Why did you marry me, Katrina? You knew of my dedication to this uniform and to the Force. Why the hell *did* you marry me?'

'Because . . . because I loved you.'

'Loved me? Past tense eh? Alles in die fokken verlede neh?'

'Yes in the past.'

'All this time I believed you loved me for what I was; what I am — a policeman. All this time I thought you also believed in the sacredness of my work.'

'Sacredness? Don't make me laugh, Andries. Low bleddy wages and long, long hours of chasing and shooting Natives who hate you and all that your uniform stands for...'

'How the fokken hell do *you* know what the Natives feel? Since when have you been talking to them?'

'Unlike you I listen to what people say. My father and mother did not spend their lives doing missionary work among the Natives for nothing. We understand them and their language. I've heard them say things about the police; bad bleddy things....'

'Hulle moere! What does a bleddy Native know? Fok die kaffers en fok jou! If you don't want me why not get out of my house?'

Dries bit his lip when the word 'kaffers' echoed through his mind. Of all the things that had embittered him towards Katrina, the worst had been her siding with the Natives against him.

'Get out is what I'm going to do Andries Swanepoel but not before I say this: I've always loathed your holy uniform which you have placed above me. Days and nights I sat alone in this bleddy house, waiting for a better life. Always duty, always serving the Volk while I struggled to exist on your poor wages.'

'You never spoke.'

'You were never around to listen, Andries. How I begged you to leave the Force but no, always "die Volk, die Volk; te hel met die Volk!" '

Dries clenched his teeth and fists as he recalled hitting her to the floor, dazed and bleeding. He spent that night in the police barracks unable to sleep. Hating her and hating himself. He volunteered for active service at the Rhodesian border with South Africa. Katrina was not home when he returned to pack his bags. Neither was she there when he came back six months later. Rumour had it that she and rugby hero Tommie Venter had absconded to Cape Town.

Gott, what a bleddy mess that was. How could a blue-blooded Afrikaner girl reject such sacred vocations as marriage and the institution embodied in his uniform? How?

Dries back-tracked to the creaking spot on the wooden floor. It always helped to stir his wife from her light slumber.

'Dries, is dit jy?'

'Ja, Liefie; wie anders.' His response was soft and reassuring. Home sweet home. A family, a place of refuge and safety, things he had not known as a child.

His thoughts raced back in time. He shuddered at the sight of the boy in his mind's eye who had watched day in and night out as all sorts of men — 'uncles' — towered and moved above his mother. How the bed shook and rattled violently while he kept watch for a father who had stopped coming home. Stopped caring.

The men had slipped money into his unbuttoned shirt the same way they slipped it under his mother's embroidered pillow-case. How one burly partner had fondled Dries between the legs and went to the bathroom for sanitation. The sound of flushing water; the hoarse throat-clearing and the clash of vomit against the wash-basin, became a sort of nightmare for the six-year-old boy. Another man. Another payment. Another flushing noise. The sound of violent gushing in the shower as his always half-drunk mother tried to scrub the shame and pain and degradation from between her legs.

Then the suicide.

The boy had watched impassively as she tied one end of a piece of curtaining rope around her neck and the other end on to the wooden beam of her ceilingless bedroom. Her eyes had searched his face. Then came a tear and a smile — the only heirlooms of a wasted and misunderstood existence lived in poverty and prostitution. What else was there to bequeath to her son? Dries recalled the thud after his mother had kicked the stool from under her feet. Blood had trickled from her nose and fell on his face and hand.

The antique clock in the hallway chimed thrice. It was not the first time that Dries Swanepoel entered his house after a whole day's absence. His wife had grown accustomed to the countless intrusions into her sleeping life; had grown accustomed to and tolerated the smell of gunpowder, sweat and blood that hung around him after security operations.

It had been a busy and violent night and a repetition of events two nights before. The whistling, the stones and the petrolbombs from those Soweto comrades had struck menacingly against the combat vehicles. Though the pelting was ineffective, the stones still drove a measure of fear into the heart. What if they had been handgrenades or rockets? What? One could never tell these days; every black man has a bomb ticking in his heart.

I must have shot and killed about ten of those bastards, thought the police hero.

'Here Gott!' The words burst out unintentionally from his well-trimmed moustached mouth. The bedroom lights went on and illuminated part of his face. His wife's voice was much stronger.

'Did you call, Dries?'

'No, I had only called on God's name. He saved me during an attack in the township. It was a dark and horrifying experience; I've never been so afraid in my life Liefie.'

'Yes . . . which township Dries?'

'Soweto, I don't kow which township. Gott, but those bloody bantus can fight.'

'Soweto? What can you expect, my husband. All that matters now is that you are home and safe.' Home and safe. The words appeared to come from a long passage in her heart. Dries entered the bedroom. She scanned his face. What a sight he was; bruised and smelling of gore.

Could this man beside her bed be the same one who, two nights ago, had carried their twins into bath water that he had softened with liquid soap and baby oil? Not too hot, not too cold; in fact not too anything for his delicate daughters. How, after tucking them in, he had prayed to God for their happiness and safe-keeping and had kissed them tenderly. And how when the house was quiet — save for the heavy breathing of lovers preparing for the sacred feast, Dries had towered over her small body. Oh how gentle was her giant then.

Empathy and love reached out of her and flooded her spouse. There was no-one in the whole wide world that mattered to her at that moment. No-one.

And yet when they had courted she had been a little afraid of the tall, hairy giant dubbed 'Bloed Bul' by his police colleagues. 'Blood Bull' was not a name she liked for it hid the gentle demeanour of a man she loved very deeply. Her strict Calvinistic upbringing had seen her through a hectic school career in which many of her best friends — male and female alike — had scorned their sleepy dorpie for the fast life of Johannesburg. Her graduation as a teacher in the Orange Free State suburb of Zastron was well-received by her traditionally conservative community. Her shopkeeper father Krisjan De Waal was also the local mayor and through his influence Liefie was appointed deputy principal of the Zastron Afrikaner Primary School. Her equally small-built mother Alena, was the matron nurse at the Phelong Hospital for black people.

Liefie grinned as she recalled how Dries Swanepoel had won her heart as she watched him play rugby at the inter-provincial police encounter at the sportsfield in her dorpie. When her hero entered the De Waal Kafee she was shaking with excitement. Dries had ordered a litre of gingerbeer and she had watched in stunned silence as he emptied the bottle without stopping to take a breath of air. Their eyes met. She did not drop her gaze but stared hard and deep into his eyes.

'Lynnette De Waal,' she had responded when Dries asked her name.

'Ag ou seun,' said her father. 'Ons noem haar net Liefie.' He stretched across the shop counter and shook Dries' hand warmly. 'Jy't goed gespeel vandag ou seun; dit was regtig 'n harde spel. De Waal, Meneer Krisjan De Waal. Ek's die burgermeester van Zastron en die vader van Liefie.' He smiled broadly and stood briefly on his toes. De Waal's ears reddened with the pride and joy of both fatherhood and authority vested in him by his Gott and his Volk. Enough to make any five-and-half-footer rise in stature. Pride did that to a man or a woman. When Dries revealed his name De Waal was quick to respond: 'Wie ken nie die Bloed Bul nie. U naam as polisie held en rugby stêr is wyd bekend ou seun.'

Dries had smiled. His reputation as police hero and rugby star appeared to follow him everywhere, thought Liefie. And how she had blushed when her father disclosed that she was an only child and a teacher.

'Pa,' she had said shyly and with all the hidden coquetry she could summon. 'Pa hoef nie my hele lewe uitlê vir vreemde mense nie.'

Dries had nodded as if in agreement. Six months later they had married and he brought her to Johannesburg. Her husband's first failure at wedlock had never changed her feelings for the feared 'Blood Bull' — a name that surely hid the gentleness and love of the man she never really knew.

That was seven years ago.

Their love-making before his departure two nights ago had, as always, been a passionate but gentle experience. Dries had come out from the bathroom naked and steaming, and as always, she was in bed waiting and willing.

Soap and water . . . would that they could reach and clean out the pain and anguish that people like Dries hid inside of them. She sighed and felt a deep throbbing in her breast on recalling how the heat of her husband's hair and body had stung into her senses. She had wanted him and touched his face. Her thin lips moved against his cheeks and like a vacuum cleaner she had tried to suck away the emptiness and dejection that had showed in his eyes. And yet he had responded to her hunger in his special way. Mutual desire breathed from their mouths and moved down to the hollow between their bodies. He had fondled her breasts, then down between her soft thighs he had felt the palpitation of her pulse beating ardently against his flesh.

Dries had entered her gently. He had moved cautiously and after what seemed like a lifetime of climbing and exploring, their worlds exploded. The smell of sweat and sulphur had pervaded her senses. And as they lay apart in the ecstasy of their consummation, Dries had breathed deeply. He had shuddered and Liefie's jaws tightened as she remembered how her hands had reached for his chest and felt the sudden change in temperature. She had rolled on top of him and held him tightly. It had not been the first such encounter. There had been nights when he cried in his sleep or gnashed his strong teeth until he bled; always calling his mother's name.

'Aah Dries; my Dries. Wat is tog fout?' she had called out to him when the police bleeper interrupted her pleading. The voice at the other end was terse and authoritative: 'Charlie Redder to Majoor Dries Swanepoel; come in.' After her husband's response, the voice gave an instruction which she had grown accustomed to since their marriage: 'Charlie Redder to Majoor Swanepoel; the situation has worsened here in Soweto. The rioters have had their ranks increased. Several township law enforcers have been shot and killed. Come to base immediately. Repeat, the situation is grave; come immediately. Over and out.'

Over and out.

Then the uniform. Then the heavy boots. Then the automatic weapons. She had watched him in silence. Then after the transformation, his parting words: 'Ek moet nou gaan werk Liefie; bid vir my,' her Dries had said.

'Ja, wees versigtig Dries,' she replied; knowing and fearing the worst.

And now he sat at the edge of the bed physically unhurt yet perhaps inwardly scathed and bruised. Who could tell?

Could this man in uniform before her be the same caring husband? What was it out there in the dark, damp and dusty streets of the black ghetto that had the power to transform men like her Dries? What was it that changed in a man that he could lift a gun and shoot down a running child with a stone in its hand? What? Could it be the smell of blood and death and burned flesh? Or the sight of people singing and dancing defiantly? Or was it the cult and cry of battle that pierced the eardrums of men and caused the blood to rush to the brain? What?

'Those bantus can be fearless at times. They kept coming and coming. We kept shooting and shooting and shooting. They attacked us from all sides with petrol bombs and stones. Some of them had guns. Blackie Swartz; you know Blackie, well he was petrol bombed and shot in the chest. It was bad, Liefie; fokken bad.'

'Is he dead?'

'Don't know but he was crying like a baby when I rescued him. Crying like a baby, Blackie Swartz was.'

There was a note of contempt in Dries Swanepoel's voice. Contempt and envy for the young soldier turned policeman, who had been seconded to the riot control division under his command. How Blackie, disobeying a command to retreat, had run wildly towards the comrades, screaming. How the reckless redhead had jumped about shooting and shouting. A petrol bomb burst against Blackie's uniform and then a bullet shattered his chest. How the comrades had whistled when he fell. The bastards had eyes in the dark.

'Are the girls all right, Liefie?'

'Yes, but they cried for you all day.'

'Ag sies tog,' said Dries, feeling deep love for his daughters.

'Dries... Dries do you think Blackie will die?'

'Ja, he's bad. He lost too much blood. Those black bastards, I must have shot and killed more than ten of them, Liefie.' He shook his head and clicked his tongue at the exaggeration. Afrikaner wives had to be impressed. The war against the enemy was for them and about their sanctity; about the children and the Volk and the land. One, ten, twelve or twenty, what did numbers matter? Dead was dead. But Gott was I scared, he told the Dries Swanepoel inside of him.

Silent thoughts. Silent fears. Everything ended in silence. The enemy is the enemy. Right kommandant, right.

'You smell of blood, Dries?'

'Ja, I know. It sits in my nose and inside my bones. But don't worry, I'll take a shower and scrub off the dirt and slime I picked up in the township.' As he spoke the wraith of his prostitute mother swung in his mind's eye. She had tried to clean the slime and stain of degradation from between her legs. Blackie Swartz's blood, and the blood and gore from the bodies of the rioters that he and his men flung into the government mortuary vehicles, had to be scrubbed off his hands. Dead was dead: one, ten, twelve or one hundred, what did it matter? There were no stains that water could not wash. His mother had shown him how....

'Liefie?'

'Ja, skat.'

'Should I dip the uniform into the bath?'

'No, leave it in the basket like always; Annah will wash it.'

'Did she come to work?'

'No. I had to fix the breakfast all by myself and even wash and feed the girls *and* empty the dirtbin.'

'But why didn't she come? She could have telephoned or something.'

'You know how it is with these people; they can lie so much.'

'Ja I know.'

'Morning, Mies Swanepoel.'

'Ja, Annah.'

'Morning, Baas Swanepoel.'

'Ja, Annah. Where were you yesterday? The mies says she had to make breakfast all by herself and even empty out the dirtbin. Where were you?'

'In the lokasie, baas, looking for my son.'

'Looking for your son?'

'Yes, baas.'

'And did you find him?'

Silence. All things ended in silence. Her youngest son Thulani, silenced by a police bullet. Then the silence which descended on the township when families searched for their sons and daughters who did not come home after a night of war between the comrades and the law enforcers. Then the silence that came with grief and burial. All things ended in silence.

'Did you find him at the police station or what?'

'No baas, in the street. They say he was shot by the police.'

'The police?'

'Yes, Mies Swanepoel, the police.'

'Which township?'

'In Chiawelo, baas. He had two holes. One in the chest, another in the head.'

Dead was dead; just like Blackie Swartz would be dead.

Majoor Dries Swanepoel looked at his wife. She stared into his grey-blue eyes and shook her head. It was not *that* possible....

'Annah?'

'Ja Mies Swanepoel?'

'Don't wash the master's uniform. I'm taking it to the dry cleaners.'

'No mies, I will wash it like always.'
'No, no Annah leave it; I'm taking it to the cleaners now.'
'I understand, Mies Swanepoel.'

CHILD OF GHAMT-GHAREB

Most of the Khoisan descendants and the Afrikaner inhabitants of Ghamt-Ghareb in the far north-western Cape accepted the birth of the albino child Sarah as a 'wonderwerk' — a miracle. But some of the more superstitious folk on both sides of the colour line swore it was a form of punishment for their own hidden sins as well as those of their dark and distant ancestors. Not in the long and uneventful history of this dry, dusty and wind-battered piece of God's earth had there been such flurries of activity nor such a wagging of tongues for what people claimed were either miracles or curses.

Ghamt-Ghareb was once situated near the pioneer town of Goodhouse in Little Bushmanland. So barren and nondescript was it, that it has never appeared on the country's maps or found its way into the pages of history books. It was named after an early Khoikhoi leader Ghamt and his wife Ghareb. Their marriage had helped to secure trade and political ties between their two tribes long before the Portuguese navigators ventured past what they called the Cape of Storms.

Centuries ago.

'This mysterious birth and the strange, persistent rain are the fulfilment of an old prophecy etched in the "Groot Boek" — the Bible, which cannot lie. It surely *is* the end of the world.' This admonition came from the tall, long-legged village crier and Kerk deacon Att van Beek, an octogenarian who, on account of his freckled face and red hair, was nicknamed Ou Rooies — Old Red. He lifted his badly tattered Dutch Bible as if it were a beacon for all to see and fear. But actually Att was shielding his tired, bloodshot eyes against the rays of the sun.

His left eye watered and as he wiped it with the sleeve of his greasy coat, Zhiem Boiys, the old shepherd, thought the grumpy deacon was crying. 'Ag diaken Rooies, djy hoef nie te huil nie. Ons glo djou darem.' After reassuring Att that they believed his prophecy and had taken heed of his admonishments, Zhiem sat and spat out the snuff he had earlier placed between his jowls. His words surprised everyone because he was known for his silence and almost fawning obedience when it came to contentious issues where he had to face the white man.

Kallie Roets, the mortician and sexton whose red pimples always appeared to be erupting like tiny volcanoes whenever he became irritated or overly excited, grinned smugly at Zhiem. That's one hotnot who knows his place, he told himself. And, as if reading the oily-faced gravedigger's mind, the shepherd spoke again — only this time somewhat louder and with a little more self-confidence. 'Wat diaken Rooies sê is maa' eenkee' tog die waa'heid. Daai keend van Dinnah en Moeraas gaa' oss amaal graf toe lei. Amaal va' oss, die Gott weet.' But Kenaas Boiys disagreed with his grandfather. He refused to believe, as the old man had emphasised, that Sarah's birth would result in the death of everyone in Ghamt-Ghareb. 'Ag, Oupa en diaken Rooies se stories en bygeloofies is skone bog en koue patats.'

Roets of course was irked by the inference that Att van Beek's warnings were nothing but idle talk as the shepherd's grandson had claimed. The sexton's thoughts raced again: These young hotnots are becoming too cheeky these days. And to show his indignation, Roets caught one of the larger volcanoes between his thumb and index finger, and pressed hard. The eruption made him wince. Tears streamed down his right cheek to mingle with the red and yellow lava. The shepherd again mistook the liquid for tears. 'Moenie huil nie Baas Roets, my klein keend praat net skone kak. Moenie huil nie.'

Embarrassed, Roets's face glowed with a redness that could have resulted in the untimely explosion of his other over-ripe pimples. Everyone looked at him curiously. He slid through their gazes and headed towards the Kerk for sanctuary from the evil that hung around him and the village. An evil that clung on to him from the mortuary where he washed and prepared the bodies of the whites for burial. No black people were allowed to work on the corpses of the Volk. Only he, Roets, whose patrilineal calling it had been since the establishment of the Boer Republic. It was a calling as sacred as soldiery and religion. Black people were not to be trusted. They had a habit of cutting off limbs and flesh for muti — medicines and charms for luck, Roets had warned when the Ghamt-Ghareb storekeeper Viljoen had suggested that blacks be employed to help him at the mortuary.

Att van Beek's audience thinned out slowly as Roets turned into the huge Kerk yard. Most of the white folk of the village believed their admonisher had become senile. Some of them took his warnings with a pinch of strong snuff — passing the pouch around in a circle until it came back to its generous owner. As a few of the snuff-takers sneezed, diaken Rooies shook his head solemnly. Soon these people of little faith would return to seek his counsel but it would be too late. There would be weeping and gnashing of teeth. Then would the trumpets sound and herald the Second Coming. This rain and that strange, almost inhuman birth of the albino child, were manifestations of the punishment and wrath of his God. Of that he was certain. He smiled at the austerity of his own thoughts. Triumphant and sure.

The shepherd's grandson grinned as the admonisher limped from the steps of the imaginary pulpit and headed towards the trading store. Such fears and superstition could be understood and even tolerated coming from the ignorant 'witmense' — the white people — but not from his own folk. Among all the tribes in Southern Africa none was as spiritually gifted as the Khoisan who had a long and profound occult tradition. How could they be so sceptical and even cynical when all the signs of miraculous occurrences had manifested themselves before their very eyes? So much rain had come to their valley after several decades of drought and disease. The neighbouring areas of Pela, Stein'skopp and Concordia were still as dry as the sands of the Kalahari. People came in their hundreds to Ghamt-Ghareb —

bringing huge drums, tins, buckets and animal-skin pouches for the miracle water.

Kenaas patted his seventy-year-old grandpa's back and pointed to the valley. 'See down there, Oupa, that is life which has come to Ghamt-Ghareb. Life that fills the rivers and the dams and makes the animals quench their thirst, and jump around and rub noses with their mates and little ones. Life. Tell me honestly, Oupa Zhiem, could such beauty — all the many colourful flowers and shrubs — be a curse? How can so much life be punishment?'

The rain, which had drizzled softly for nearly two hours, began to fall again. The shepherd's woolly grey hair soaked the raindrops and glistened when the sun emerged briefly from behind the dark clouds that hung over the village. Water dripped down Zhiem's neck and on to his back. It was the closest he had ever come to having a bath, and when Kenaas teased him about it, Zhiem lashed at him with a long whip and spat a ball of snuff at the fleeing boy.

'Life? Life se moer. Dis sommaa' nonsins daai life. Skone kak as djy my vra. Skone bleddie kak!'

The rain fell harder.

Kenaas was correct. The sleepy village had been transformed into a kind of mini carnival with the influx of hundreds of visitors and water-seekers — many of them simply inquisitive folk who merely wanted to see and experience the miracles for themselves. Three weeks of continuous and persistent rain — but for the single two-hour break — enough to set the tongues wagging. It had all begun the moment the resident white midwife, Sarah de Leeuw, gently smacked the albino infant's backside. The loud screams that had followed the gentle assault were to tear the celestial curtains asunder. Booming thunder, preceded by white, snake-like flashes of lightning, echoed through the valley. Both man and animal had to run helter-skelter when the heavy drops pounded the dry soil and the shrubs and trees. Dinnah, the child's mother, had cried softly, still not believing that it was happening to her. There had been fears for Dinnah's life because of her age. But when the midwife — after whom the child was named — told her 'Alles is reg ou meid,' her fears vanished. If 'Mies' Sarah said all was well, who was she to doubt? The white people were knowledgeable in these matters, Dinnah thought.

When she saw how pallid Sarah's skin was, Dinnah drew her breath in sharply. The midwife smiled reassuringly. 'There's no mistake. It *is* your baby, Dinnah — white as flour. Perhaps when she grows up in this hot place — this hot oven, she might become brown like bread and we could all have a slice of her,' said Sarah de Leeuw whose laughter was as soft and gentle as her hands. Hands that had helped many women — white and black — bring their children into the world. Her only child — a girl — had died an hour after birth. Several miscarriages had followed and midwifery gave her the opportunity to be near to the child-bearing experience. She was grateful for that.

In many ways her work filled the gap of loneliness that had plagued her for several years. Most of the villagers loved and respected her. She had told Dinnah that the child was an albino — a 'wit kaffertjie' — a white 'kaffir' as some of the more coarse and lewd Afrikaners called albinos. The blacks too used the term to describe their pink-skinned counterparts. The midwife's chief concern was having to deliver the child of a fifty-five-year-old woman. A fear that was shared by the university-trained geneticist Wilhelminah Visagie, who had received the news of Dinnah's pregnancy with disbelief. Her incredulity was compounded by the fact that Dinnah had experienced her change-of-life at the age of forty-eight years — accompanied by an illness which Wilhelminah had treated. That was seven years ago, when she worked as a gynaecologist at a hospital near Goodhouse.

When Moeraas, the baby's father, heard the first cry from outside the local white clinic, he went to pee. He shuddered several times, then shook his head. 'Gott Dinnah,' was all he could say. It was traumatic and frightening for a man to become a father at fifty-nine.'Here Gott,' he exclaimed and found solace in invoking God's name. There was no profanity. Only the incomprehensibility of the experience, and the inexplicable sense of bewilderment that filled his heart. Moeraas tried to count his age on his shaky fingers. A smile crossed his face and his narrow eyes closed completely. Joy and pride welled up inside him to evoke a strength he never realised he possessed. Tears gathered in his eyes and flooded the banks of his cheeks; a mighty river flooding the fields of doubt and scepticism. He Moeraas, a father after so many years of waiting.

Years of prayer and supplication. Years of being mocked and teased by men and women alike for being impotent. A bull without testicles. Now other men would look at him and say: 'Daar loop 'n man; 'n regte bul. . . .' The thought of him being a real man — a bull, made Moeraas click his tongue after the fashion of his Khoisan forebears.

The rain fell harder as Zhiem Boiys fawningly greeted 'Baas' Alwie du Pont, the chairman of the Sheep Shearers' Association of Ghamt-Ghareb. Du Pont nodded and filled his glass with another shot of brandy. He stretched his legs luxuriously on his verandah and gazed onto the west earth. His heavily bearded mouth opened and he swallowed the liquor without blinking. Born and bred in the Little Bushmanland-Namakwaland area seventy years ago, he mused on the fact that he could still take a full glass of brandy in a single swill without so much as a cough or a gasp. Lightning snaked in the twilight sky followed by the cracking sound of thunder.

'Where the hell have you heard of such lightning and thunder in Klein Boesmanland? People everywhere have been talking nonsense about this sudden rainfall — claiming that it is a miracle.' Du Pont's voice was muffled by the deep rumbling which echoed through the valley. His grandson, Klein Alwie interjected: 'Oupa, is it true that outah Moeraas and his wife got a white baby? All the outahs and our people are talking and making jokes about it,' said the boy, biting into a piece of biltong.

'What do they say?'

'Who? Does oupa mean the Boesmans?'

'Yes, boy,' somewhat irritated. 'I *do* mean them.'

'Well they reckon that Dinnah has been sleeping with white men because according to them Moeraas has no manhood.' The boy spoke nonchalantly and prised a splinter of wood between his teeth to extract a few strands of meat.

'Skone kak!' shouted Du Pont and turned his back. 'Go to bed. It's getting late. And don't forget to pray, klein mistertjie,' he said warmly.

'But oupa since when do I have to go to bed so early?' protested the boy. He was intelligent and observant beyond his ten years.

Du Pont's only grandson, he had won a very special place in the sheep farmer's heart. The boy's agility and mischievousness also made him a favourite among the inhabitants of Ghamt-Ghareb. He jumped on a wooden chair, kissed his grandfather full on the mouth and after sniffing like a dog would, he said 'Nag oupa,' and climbed off the chair.

'Oupa?' he called out questioningly.

'Ja,' came a deliberately slow response, 'wat's fout my seun?'

'Is oupa alweer dronk?' And without waiting for a reply, the boy vanished into the house.

Just then Moeraas greeted: 'Nag, baas Pont.'

'Nag outah,' he responded and enquired after Dinnah's health and whether it was true that their baby was white.

'As white as snow with eyes that roll and roll and roll,' he replied in Afrikaans. He had not called the farmer 'baas' again. It struck Moeraas that Du Pont too had noticed the omission and nodded. His grandson's words about the white men who were said to have slept with Dinnah, shot through his mind.

'Skone kak,' he exclaimed — not aiming the words at Moeraas.

He replied indignantly: 'Wonderwerk is al wat ek en my Dinnah kan sê.'

Bright flashes of lightning again lit the sky and the stubborn thunder growled in response. Du Pont poured more brandy into his glass. The contents slid down his throat and warmed his stomach briefly. The last word was his: 'Skone kak!'

Everyone had been baffled by Dinnah's pregnancy, especially Wilhelminah Visagie whose father owned the only trading store in the village. She had compiled a report for the university complete with photographs of the couple. There appeared to be no biologically scientific explanation other than to record that Dinnah's maternal ancestors — including her mother — had all conceived their children in their mid or late fifties. A type of hereditary phenomenon.

Mietah Bloem, the Visagie family's faithful domestic worker of about forty years, had told the geneticist that the pregnancy, the birth and the rain were all part of the great miracle of Ghamt-Ghareb. Mietah had raised the Visagie boys, Anton and Frans who had died in battles at Alamein and Tripoli during the Second World War. Wilhelminah's mother Magriet, crippled by a stroke after the deaths of her sons, had been overjoyed at the news of Dinnah's pregnancy, and had ordered Mietah to give money, food, clothes and bedding.

'It *is* a miracle. Gott has blessed our village with so much rain after the birth of the child,' said Magriet Visagie. Mietah agreed. 'A real wonderwerk, this white baby of Suster Dinnah,' she said.

'Not a white baby, Mietah, but an albino — and it's not a miracle. Albinos are born every day — it's got something to do with the blood,' interjected the geneticist, deciding not to argue or explain the intricacies of her profession to her audience.

'Perhaps these albinos are born every day in your book, but it is not every day that a fifty-five-year-old woman gives birth, Wilhelminah. Sy's 'n regte wit vroutjie daai keend van Dinnah.' The remark sealed the conversation. The geneticist lowered her head into a thick science book.

Many farm labourers from Okiep and Pofadder also travelled to Ghamt-Ghareb to witness the miracle of the persistent life-giving rain and visit Dinnah and Moeraas and their milk-faced baby with the rolling eyes. The great traffic of people into the village meant more business for Visagie, the broad-shouldered storekeeper who had been a Smuts man — Red Tabs and all — until the fateful 1948 elections. The strong Broeder Movement of the Afrikaners had transformed the country as well as the lives of the ordinary Boers. Visagie's own family — his father, his uncles and his mother's people were divided by the rise of the Afrikaner nationalists. Open hostilities had developed to a point where the Visagie clan split — some to stay with General Smuts and the majority to follow Malan.

The division was begun when his two eldest sons joined the Union Defence Force as soldiers of the Allied Forces during the Second World War. Both of them died. Ironically many of Visagie's relatives — among them his eldest brother — joined and colluded with the Afrikaner Ossewa Brandwag, the movement against the government of General Smuts and the British allies who operated bases from South Africa during the war. The storekeeper's support for Smuts continued up to the 1948 elections when he switched sides to support the fiery Afrikaner nationalists. Since then he had never looked back.

'Gott gives and Gott takes,' Visagie had said in the Groot Kerk when news of his sons' deaths reached him in 1941. Even the Brandwag people came to support his family during that bereavement which crippled his wife. The Boers had stood by him just as he had supported and fed their families during the dreaded Koffiefontein Internee Camp incarcerations of Nazi sympathisers. After that contribution the Brandwag people tolerated him. They would finally accept and trust him only when he was one of them; one of the Volk whose calling and mission was to establish a new land under Gott — purified and prepared for sacrifice and nationhood. Now he was a true nationalist, respected by white and black alike for his sense of fair play and compassion. The growing support he got from people outside his tribe and culture was proof of his popularity among the black people. This Visagie believed with all his heart.

Visagie's silver vintage cash register with its artistically carved designs was specifically serviced for the influx of new business. Impressive photographs of his war-hero sons were pasted on it. Business boomed since the coming of the albino baby. People actually ordered Coca-Cola and melktert. Most of them were the inquisitive and noisy 'dorpsmense' — city dwellers. One could see from their manner of dress and their brashness. Their women used thick make-up and wore short, low-neckline dresses, the village women complained. But the local males swooned and fell over their feet just watching the new visitors. The rain didn't help to cool temperatures either. Visagie smiled and told Kallie Roets that it was good for business. Roets disagreed although just looking at the city women brought a warm feeling between his legs.

'Dorpsmense, Coke and melktert,' said Roets, counting on his fingers his version of the three deadly sins. 'Gott, our klein ou dorpie is going mad; skone befok as jy my vra.' He had only come to the store to have a peep before heading for his room behind the Kerk to scrub the smell of dead bodies off his hands. He unlocked the door of his house and cursed anew. 'Hierdie dorpsvrouens is net skone laf,' he said, rubbing his greasy and pimpled face on the dirty towel behind the wooden door. The towel moved violently across his face — losing a few of its fibres because of the force with which Roets performed the ritual. The mortician stared into the cracked mirror and saw many reflections of himself. He pulled faces and after applying oil to his hair, produced a comb from his back trousers pocket and disciplined his hair. The comb returned to its resting place. The funeral service was complete.

'Gott Roets,' he said addressing his mirror-self. 'You really *are* a proud jentilmin — soos die Rooinekke sou sê.' An index finger went into his mouth, collected some saliva and rubbed it against his eyebrows, smearing them into place. A boyishly deceptive smile lit up his face. His green eyes added lustre to his greasy, pimpled skin and he licked his lips. Mental photographs of the city women with their low necklines and heaving breasts developed from the negatives of his mind. The women in front of him — stark naked and waiting. His hand reached down between his thighs: 'If only I could get one of them for the night. Jislaaik! It would be enought to melt *all* those bodies in the Goodhouse mortuary. Just think of it — Kallie Roets on top of one of those losmeide.' He looked at his twin in the mirror which appeared to say: 'That will be the fokken day....'

Roets remembered the albino child and the persistent and irritating rain that had nearly drowned him while he supervised the grave-digging for Boet de Jongh who had died on his honeymoon at a Cape Town hotel. He laughed quietly as he thought about the incident. 'Aai regtig,' he said aloud. 'Ou Boet just couldn't take that final bend. One kick on the starter and his battery just packed in. If it was me, Hester would still have been singing "Happy days are here again." ' Roets found strength in his wishful thoughts. The smell of the corpses still hung heavily around him. Stubborn and strong. His mirror-self spoke to him: 'You can't wash death from your hands, Roets like you do the soil of the grave. Death lives and moves with you constantly. In the dark or lighted alleys of your life. A second self. Stubborn and strong. Waiting to snatch and pull you down. Roets you cannot wash death from your hands....'

The mortician shook out of his reverie — shocked by his thoughts. He flung the wet towel at the mirror which fell and cracked to pieces.

He left his room and headed for the trading store. The place was overcrowded and the heat reached out to touch him. The smell of brandy and Coca-Cola gave a warmth to the atmosphere as the people jostled and pushed each other. The black people bought their goods at a small window underneath a canopy that Visagie had specially built out to shield them from the rain. His youngest son Andries served them liquor on the sly and shared the fun of their giggling and laughter. There was something about the laughter of these people, thought Andries, that drew a man to them. It was a sort of reckless abandon — like the white spray of the sea against the waiting rocks. A scene he witnessed in Cape Town while on holiday. How he had marvelled at the water — rushing madly to splash into a million pieces, only to re-collect and rush back to its source. The laughter of the black people was like that — they gave all yet took it back to themselves in the end.

Roets ordered melktert and ginger beer. As he lifted the bottle to his mouth, he stared at a blonde out of the corner of his eye. For a night — only for one bloody night. His throat moved twice. The gingerbeer vanished. A real proud jentilmin. At that point, deafening thunder bellowed over the valley and shook the ground. A heavier downpour than previously experienced appeared to be falling from a hole in the sky. It became pitch dark — at only four in the afternoon. The rain soaked into the skins of human and animal.

Diaken Att van Beek, who relished a bottle of wine now and then, told his neighbour and friend of many years, Nic Waterboer, that both the drought and the sudden rain were curses and signs of God's wrath.

'This rain is a clear message from the Almighty. The end of the world is at hand. Do you hear me, Nic — the end.'

The arid wasteland drank its fill and sucked the precious drops into an invisible sponge to soak the life-grains at the inner, unreachable depths of the earth. Deep and hard. And the earth burst her bowels and gave life to the slumbering roots of the shrubs and the trees and the plants. A carpet of multi-coloured flowers sprouted to beautify the wasteland and salute the world. It was Nature's way of showing her might and majesty over puny man. Rain to the earth. Life to the trees, the shrubs and the plants.

The balance was struck....

The resident traditional herbal doctor and spiritual leader of the Khoisan descendants in Little Bushmanland, Gharoeb Ghatooma, clicked his tongue in triumph and inner satisfaction. That one prophecy — among the many he had made over the years — had finally realised itself although not to the letter and spirit of his dreams and oral predictions. For there were some crucial elements missing. Missing was that mysterious and ominous cloud that had hung over his head and had reappeared several times bearing the effigy of someone he felt he knew. A face shaped almost like his own but whose eyes had been gouged from their sockets. Mysterious and frightening. The child came and the rain followed. He Gharoeb, the chosen of his people, had used all his powers and prayers, rituals and psychic training — taught and bequeathed to him by generations and generations of Khoisan forebears, to try and unravel the mystery of the gouged eyes. But to no avail. And although he had resigned himself to the oracle, the unease remained. In desperation he had sought the counsel of his wise mentor and spiritual leader, Thaan-oopi in the hope that the haunting dream would be revealed to him.

The wise Thaan-oopi had clicked his tongue in eager salutation when the mentally and spiritually uneasy Gharoeb called on him in the Kalaghari. Their embrace was firm and warm and brought smiles and grins to their wrinkled faces. Thaan-oopi, a direct descendant of the Mbanderu tribe, was more than a hundred years old. His people had travelled with the dominant Herero from the then Bechuanaland (now Botswana) to South West Africa to an area controlled by the Namas. The nomads were given free access to the waterhole and grazing land. But the Mbanderu-Herero youth abused the hospitality of their hosts whose womenfolk they attacked and raped. A fierce and bloody battle ensued and the Herero-Mbanderu warriors massacred the Namas — but they lost many of their own soldiers who included the twelve-year-old Thaan-oopi's diviner and herbal-healer father, Mbanderu Thaan. Thirty years later Thaan-oopi's mother Thirru and his sisters were killed by an army of avenging Namas who slaughtered hundreds of Hereros at a place called Okahandja. It was there that Thaan-oopi set up his practice under the watchful eye of his uncle Rihimba Thaan. It was not long and Thaan-oopi earned the love and respect of the Herero and Khoisan people who had to trek for several days to be treated for their ailments. It was also at the royal village of Okahandja that the Herero revolted against the German colonisers.

'It was a great war, Gharoeb. The white settlers who had taken the land and all its rich minerals, had ordered our people not to worship Ndjambi Karunga, the Supreme Being, but to pray in the white churches. The Germans controlled our movements and impounded our waterholes, taking away our rich grazing lands. Our farmers were dragged before their courts for failing to pay debts they had imposed on our people,' said Thaan-oopi without a croak in his voice.

Gharoeb clicked empathetically.

'Those problems still exist in our land, Thaan-oopi. To this very day the war between the settlers and our people continues. I fear that it will never end,' said Gharoeb with deep resignation.

'It will end, my son. Nothing is forever save the spirit that moves within us. We too cannot live forever, Gharoeb. As the rain will come to Ghamt-Ghareb when the rolling eyes open, so too will end the fears and anguish of Ghatooma the chosen one,' said Thaan-oopi sombrely.

Gharoeb, who was filled with profound disquiet, clicked his tongue several times. He stood up and walked from his teacher's dwelling and headed towards a high sand dune. The wind rolled over the sand and made beautiful waves — like the flowing mane of a Barbary sheep. He pondered long on Thaan-oopi's words. What would the future be? Back in the dwelling the tale of the Herero rebellion was taken up again when Gharoeb squatted before his spiritual mentor.

'Much blood was spilled but we overpowered the foreigners. They lost hundreds of their soldiers. For three long hard years our warriors kept them at bay but with the support of a strong Boer mercenary force aided by black traitors they defeated us. Hundreds of our people — men, women and children — were herded into camps and special prisons. I was wounded and left for dead,' said Thaan-oopi.

Gharoeb clicked his tongue. It was a tale he had heard as a child, but never so vividly related; never from one who had actually fought against the Germans. In the tradition of his forebears, the chosen one of Ghamt-Ghareb placed a sheepskin pouch in front of Thaan-oopi. No talking accompanied the ritual, only the deft movement of the hands, the blinking of the ever-watchful eyes, and the slow mumbling of the lips in prayers and solicitation. What was inside — the fears, the hopes, the dreams and the uncertainty — would be carried in the silent corridors of the soul, to be uttered only in the presence of people like Thaan-oopi of the Mbanderu. When the wise one of the Kalahari was physically no more, he Gharoeb would stand in his shadow and his spirit to perpetuate the culture and the histories of the Khoikhoi, the San and the Mbanderu, whose God Ndjambi Karunga was One with their Tixo.

For was it not Gharoeb's father Xhima Ghatooma who had found the injured Thaan-oopi in the Water Mountain surrounded by several vultures and hyenas? The scavengers, according to Gharoeb's father, appeared to be protecting the crippled fugitive. The tale had made Thaan-oopi a legend in the Kalahari. It was on the insistence of Xhima that the quietly spoken Gharoeb should live with and be trained by Thaan-oopi. It was during the initiation rituals of blood, salt and snuff that he had seen a darkness in the eyes of the young Gharoeb. Thaan-oopi knew that some deeper secrets would remain hidden to his charge. Yet not to him, the diviner of the Mbanderu. He could see all. There would be the murder of a man after whose wife Gharoeb would lust. There would be the secret burial place of the man's body, and dogs that would dig up the head with the gouged out eyes. A crime which the chosen one would carry in his heart and so suffer the loss of his powers of healing and prophecy until the manifestation of the miracles of Ghamt-Ghareb. Then would the hour of retribution come for the life that was taken. Only he, Thaan-oopi, knew that.

He clicked his tongue when the chosen one left the dwelling in the Kalaghari wasteland. 'Go, Gharoeb of the troubled spirit. Go and meet your destiny,' Thaan-oopi had said as his charge vanished behind the rolling, restless dunes.

It was a reunion that the wise one had relished with the

fervour of olden times. Their communicative clicking had extended into the early hours of morning. Two gifted men sharing the secrets of one of Africa's most ancient peoples. Secrets that had withstood the scepticism and disbelief which the settlers brought with them from across the great waters. Waters that divided not only the continents, but also the customs, traditions, the cultures and the hearts of men.

Gharoeb had told the simple folk of his village of the miracle that would come through the withered womb and from the tired loins of a man who had lost his manhood and the respect of other men. He told them of the rain that would bless Ghamt-Ghareb. The people had at first believed him but as the years went by they became rude and nasty. The Boers teased and belittled him in the presence of his followers whose children in turn also laughed and scoffed at him. Sometimes the children circled round and sang a ditty whose words undermined his status as their spiritual leader:

> Gharoeb, Gharoeb
> Hy's vol drome
> En vol poep!

The ditty made fun of him, saying he was a dreamer full of fart. Men had stopped buying his herbal medicines and aphrodisiacs. The women also kept away — no longer seeking his wisdom and counselling; no longer buying potions for the winning of men's hearts or for the bearing of children. The bottles and tins in his dispensary had remained untouched and unsought for many years. This time, this one very last time .... The thought stuck in his mind and the words echoed: This last time. What did this mean?

Only two of his followers — Dinnah his relative and her husband Moeraas, had believed the prophecy and had never laughed at him. The couple had regularly visited his shack and taken his fertility potions without question. For more than thirty years Dinnah, whose father Ghariem was the son of Gharoeb's paternal uncle, gave money and food to her dejected diviner kin.

Twenty years before meeting Moeraas, Dinnah was the wife of the handsome and physically strong Khimati Worrah who was shot and killed by Jaap Greyling, the horse-breeder from Pofadder, barely two months after his marriage to Dinnah. How the people had talked. One of the farmhands, Giep, had told Gharoeb that Greyling had found the good-looking stable-hand in his bedroom where his wife slept. She had screamed hysterically when several shots were fired into Khimati's body. Nothing had come of the case. It was a matter of self-defence. Of honour. It was Gharoeb who brought Moeraas from the Kalaghari to wed the grieving Dinnah who had stood by him, faithful, obedient.

Thirty-five years passed and then came the fulfilment of his prophecy. In the glow of candlelight, he had told Dinnah and Moeraas of the child with the milk face and the rolling eyes. And the coming of the rain. The long, long rain that would restore his standing among his people, and so bring them closer to the ancestors and to the Mighty Tixo who spoke to him in his dreams. Spoke, yet did not reveal all.

Gharoeb headed towards Dinnah's shack bearing gifts of food, clothes and money. She had returned from the white clinic where she was allowed to give birth. If ever there was a miracle, then that was it — allowing Dinnah to have her baby at the clinic. Aaaiii! But the Boers are strange creatures, thought Gharoeb and clicked his tongue.

The Visagie family and the local midwife had had long meetings with the other Afrikaner leaders and Kerk elders of the village about allowing Dinnah the use of the white clinic. There was near pandemonium at the first gathering when Visagie's suggestion almost brought the roof of the Kerk down. Everyone had reacted simultaneously — like a huge volcano surging up to spew its venom on the sleepy village. The din and noise rattled Visagie's crippled wife. Hurt and disappointed that her spouse's suggestion could cause so much shouting, she rose from the makeshift wheelchair to the open astonishment of all, and walked to the pulpit.

'If we say that we are Christians, then surely we must allow the woman Dinnah to have her baby at our clinic.' Stunned by her own feat, she collapsed. A deep silence prevailed. One woman shouted: 'Praise Gott vir die wonderwerk!' A miracle before their eyes. Surely Gott, the Gott of their fathers and of their nation, was speaking to them through Suster Magriet Visagie. Surely.

Att van Beek — not to be left behind, shouted: 'It's the end of the world! Surely it *is* the end of the world!'

A deep silence fell over the congregation.

Sarah, the child with the milk face and the rolling eyes, came as he Gharoeb the chosen, had foretold. He shook his head and clicked his tongue. They had all returned to seek his counsel and wisdom — white and black folk alike. The whites called him to their homes in the dead of night — afraid that their neighbours would smell them out. Gharoeb made a lot of money in the three weeks that the rain fell. More than he could ever spend. He walked tall. Tall and confident. Confidence and triumph, how they can swell a man's heart and his chest.

If it was a time for miracles and the softening of hearts, then it was also a time for scepticism and jocular derision from among the young Boers who teased their elders. Dries Kotze whose father owned a huge karakul goat farm in the village, said: 'Pa, I just hope those Rooinek dorpsmense won't use this "white child" story to get at our people and cause another general election scandal. Smuts was a bad loser and who knows what he's got up his sleeve.' The remark was a facetious one aimed at pulling his father's leg.

Lennart Langtong Botha, who was visiting at the Kotze farm specifically to see Maria, Dries's sister, laughed aloud. 'You are right, ou Dries. Before you know it those Joodse newspaper reporters will be writing big "skinder" stories about sex across the colour line. A wit kind here and a wit kind there, and a wit kind, wit kind every bleddie where!'

Albertus didn't like his son's jokes nor Langtong's teasing. He got up from his chair and pushed his son against a wall. 'Listen, don't ever make such stupid statements about the general election. It was a sacred victory for our people.'

But Langtong interjected: 'Dries is correct, Oom Albertus. Those Rooinekke could easily accuse Oom of crossing your sheep with goats, you know. Jislaaik, just think of it: sex across the sheep line!' Dries burst out laughing as his father left the room.

'Making jokes about such serious matters is more than I can take,' said Albertus Kotze angrily.

'Ag, dis net 'n grap oom,' shouted Langtong as his prospective father-in-law walked into the rain.

Gharoeb heard their voices as he passed the Kotze house.

Langtong noticed him and jabbed Dries in the ribs. 'Jy beter jou bek hou, swaer, daai Gharoeb is 'n kafferdokter hoor. Hy maak nou jou gevreet pikswart. Pasop boetie of jy gaan die swart skaapie van die Kotze familie wees!' He cleared his throat and spat at Gharoeb's feet.

The chosen one turned round to look at the tall wiry auctioneer, and shook his head. No wonder they call him Langtong, thought Gharoeb, only with a name like that could he spit so far. He resumed his pilgrimage to the albino child's manger.

The rain fell harder.

Gharoeb was not the only person on a goodwill mission. For two weeks Dinnah's shack had witnessed the comings and goings of many concerned, compassionate and curious people — mostly Afrikaner women and their daughters who brought gifts of blankets, food, money and clothes for the infant. The dominee's wife Kristine, for whom Dinnah had washed and ironed before and during her pregnancy, gave sheets and blankets. Maarten 'Sweep' Minnaar, the brash, no-nonsense poultry farmer, donated the tar and sacking he had purchased for his own use. He had even ordered his workers to patch the leaking roof of Dinnah's shack.

'Nog 'n miracle,' the bewildered farmhands exclaimed when ordered to fix the roof.

Gharoeb clicked his tongue and scratched his head. It was indeed a time for miracles. The bad had to be taken with the good.

As the diviner advanced towards the door of Dinnah's shack a violent bolt of lightning struck above his head and lit up the sky. He could see the houses and shops behind him. A chill fell on his shoulders and travelled down his spine. His toes were numbed. Then came the thunder — hoarse and booming against his eardrums. Something bad was in the air. The dark face with the gouged eye sockets flashed rapidly before him. The fingers of his left hand felt cold and he clenched his fist. A prickly sensation moved through his arm and stopped at his heart. What did it all portend?

When Gharoeb entered the shack Moeraas noticed that his oval face, always a strong apricot brown, was ashen. The attractively narrow eyes were wide open and vacant — a mixture of fright and bewilderment. Dinnah too stared hard at Gharoeb and simultaneously pressed her hand against her baby's eyes. Why? And as if reading their minds, he nodded his silent assurance in tr spiritual leader. He dropped a bag on to the bed and placed several pound notes near the child's pillow.

'And this is for the child with the milk face and the rolling eyes, and for your faith in me and in the Great Spirit that directs our lives and causes death.'

Moeraas nodded in quiet deference to a man for whom he harboured an inexplicable fear. He clicked his tongue in gratitude — aware of his wife's unwavering faith and trust in the man. Of all the gifts he and his Dinnah had received from the many well-wishers in Ghamt-Ghareb and from areas surrounding their village, none would be more prized and cherished. For was Gharoeb not the chosen one who communed with the spirits and healed the afflictions of the body and of the spirit?

Moeraas's eyes moved from the spiritual leader to his wife and to the baby that sucked on her. A real 'wit vroutjie'. The spectacle of mother and child still baffled him as had the news of her pregnancy. Then the swelling and the clumsy gait — like a drunk person moving from side to side — which had set the village agog with gossip.

'Gits, Dinnah,' Moeraas had said, 'wat die hel gaan nou aan? Is djy seker, ou meid?' But Dinnah had known from the strange feeling inside her that Gharoeb the chosen — the last of a special breed of gifted descendants of her people the San and the Khoikhoi — had helped to restore her womanhood. Three weeks of life-giving rain and countless acts of charity and kindness were not needed to convince her of Gharoeb's supernatural powers and his prophethood.

There was silence between them. Sarah's father could hear his heart beating fast against his chest. He too had seen that blinding flash of lightning, heard the deafening thunder roar like a forest of lions and seen the fear in the diviner's eyes. He cleared his throat and coughed. 'See it is still raining hard, Gharoeb; the miracle is not ended,' said Moeraas in an attempt to get the pensive Gharoeb to speak.

'Yes, it is raining, but it will stop,' said the diviner.

'Stop? Rain such as this should fall forever. It is so blessed,' said Moeraas. He looked to his wife for support. Dinnah read her husband's thoughts.

'Yes wise one, why must such blessing and peace come to an end before all have acclaimed the miracles which you foretold, or shared the new life which has come to our village?'

In all her days, she had never spoken so eloquently. Moeraas was touched. How frail she had become. Not in all the years had he felt so much love, so much compassion for her as during the long ordeal of her pregnancy and the birth of their child. Inside himself, in that place where the seeds of remorse and penance lie dormant because the lips have been hardened by foolish pride and stubbornness, Moeraas promised himself never again to hurt his Dinnah. Never again.

Gharoeb remained silent. The wrinkles on his forehead multiplied and criss-crossed when he frowned. His thin, strong lips moved: 'I hear you Dinnah, blood of my blood. Your words lie warm and deep in my soul. Yet did you not see the lightning and hear the voice of the Great Spirit? Surely you are not so blind as not to know what these signs mean?'

'I saw and heard, Gharoeb,' interjected Moeraas, speaking in a whisper. 'But my Dinnah, though of your flesh and blood, was not endowed with your spiritual insight; how would she know?'

His wife nodded. 'Moeraas is correct, Gharoeb. It was not given to me to comprehend the ways of our spiritual forebears. Often I have wondered why it was so; why I should feel so much within me yet have not the power to cure or to understand fully the history and culture of our ancestors. But this much I do know: there is something good here. Your prophecy has been fulfilled despite the scepticism and disbelief of the white and black people of Ghamt-Ghareb. You *are* the chosen one.'

Gharoeb smiled and clicked his tongue. 'You are right, Dinnah. I should not have expected you to comprehend that which is hidden even to me.' His thoughts were of the dark face with the gouged out eyes.

'Yes, my children, I have seen the miracles. I watched the orange, red, yellow, white and purple flowers raise their heads towards the Great Spirit in gratitude for the healing rain. I saw dry dams and rivers swell and flow and give life to shrubs and trees which in turn gave me herbs with which to heal the bodies and spirits of others.'

He walked towards the rickety bed to watch the albino child suck on Dinnah. His eyes widened and he smiled: the child with the milk face and the rolling eyes. Thaan-oopi's words echoed in his mind: 'It will end, my son. Nothing is for ever save the Spirit that moves within us .... As the rain will come to Ghamt-Ghareb when the rolling eyes open, so too will end the fears of Ghatooma the chosen one.'

Sombre words heavy with foreboding.

Moeraas spoke: 'Gharoeb, I too have witnessed miracles. I heard the Boere sing in their Kerk "Die Here is goed". There is a gentleness in their manner and in their eyes when they speak to our people. Many of them — previously hard and cruel to our people — now show humaneness and concern for our children. These are miracles in themselves.'

Dinnah again supported her husband. 'Moeraas is correct. Something great has come to pass in our village.' Gharoeb turned to look at Moeraas. 'Then you agree, Moeraas. You who have always nodded your acquiescence yet carried the thorns of doubt in your heart — saying yes to my prophecy only to please your wife.'

'It is as you say, Gharoeb. But I am a changed man. For surely there is a miracle in this very room. You *are* the chosen one; the mouth through which the ancestors speak and the prophet through whom the Great Spirit manifests Himself.'

'Forgive us,' said Dinnah.

'There is nothing to forgive,' Gharoeb said and smiled. But his fears returned when he looked at the child. Dinnah felt the vibrations. 'And the child, what will become of our Sarah?' she asked. Moeraas searched the diviner's face. The older man shook his head and then left the shack, closing the door behind him. More lightning flashed. Thunder boomed. The hollowed-out eye sockets stared at Gharoeb. Long and hard. His face became pale and heavy with brooding thoughts. Thick drops of rain soaked into his hair and clothes. Gharoeb knew that there was dirt and stain which the rain could not wash away. The dirt and sin of a crime locked in his soul. The shadow of the man he had murdered followed him even in his dreams.

Moeraas ran out and shouted: 'Gharoeb! Gharoeb! What about the child? What about our little Sarah?'

The shouting was clear even amid the noise of the rain and the thunder. Gharoeb replied: 'The rain will stop. The rolling eyes will roll no more when the little heart rests and sleeps,

Moeraas.' Filled with anxiety the child's father ran back to his shack. Dinnah's eyes pierced him. He touched the child's face. There was warmth and there was life. In all his fifty-nine years on earth he had not felt so much love in his heart. Dinnah lifted the child and gave it suck. A new strength filled Moeraas.

Long after midnight Moeraas was awakened by bright flashes of lightning and roaring thunder. Sarah gave one sharp cry that shook Dinnah. A coldness crept into her breasts. She opened the blanket and saw that her child's eyes were wide open. There was no movement in them — only a blankness. The same terrifying blankness she had seen in Gharoeb's face. Sarah's lips and cheeks turned blue. Dinnah screamed: 'Moeraas! Moeraas! Die keend, die keend!'

Her husband rose from his bed on the floor and touched his daughter's face. In blind anxiety he ran outside and headed for Gharoeb's dwelling. The rain stopped as suddenly as it had started exactly three weeks ago to the day. A hush fell over Ghamt-Ghareb. People came out of their houses and shacks and held out their hands. Kallie Roets nodded approvingly — at last the long, pestering and cumbersome rain had stopped. Members of the Visagie family, dressed in pyjamas and dressing gowns, came out to investigate. Magriet was helped by Mietah and Wilhelminah as she nestled into a chair on the verandah. ''n Ware wonderwerk,' she exclaimed. Her husband went down on his knees and embraced her tenderly, satisfied that he too had witnessed miracles. Ghamt-Ghareb *was* indeed the village of his heart. Blessed and cherished.

Diaken Rooies lifted his tattered bible and walked towards the Kerk. 'Surely this *is* another sign from God. Another curse. Surely!' he exclaimed for all to hear.

Dinnah prayed with quiet resignation: 'Die Here shee en die Here vat.'

Lennart Botha — whose reputation as a master auctioneer in the Northern and Eastern Cape had earned him the name of 'Langtong' — emerged half drunk and looked at the sky. It was unusually dark for five in the morning. He held out his long, bony hand, cleared his throat and spat into the mud. 'Miracle se moer,' he said aloud and returned to his room.

Moeraas cried bitterly. 'Gharoeb will answer to me. How cruel to give a man something as precious as a child after so many years of waiting, praying and believing, then to take it away again. I will *make* him answer. Gharoeb, Gharoeb,' he shouted at the diviner's shack. 'It is me, Moeraas. The rain has stopped just as you said it would. And Sarah, my little Sarah....'

The words choked in his sobbing. Anger and pain pulled at his heart. He pushed the door ajar and again called out his spiritual leader's name. There was no reply. The room was dark. It had a pungent odour of wild herbs. The darkness changed his anger to foreboding. Momentarily immobilised, he thought of the time Gharoeb had confronted him about his scepticism and heavy drinking. How the diviner's eyes had burned into him at the time and sent cold shivers through his body. He had tried to hit at Gharoeb but missed and fell. He was pinned down by Gharoeb whose hands closed around his throat and almost choked him to death. Dinnah had intervened and pleaded with the diviner to spare his life. What strength he had felt in the older man's hands! What fear had shot through his body when the spiritual leader's eyes pierced through him! This time, this time Gharoeb would answer to him.

Moeraas found and lit a candle. His shadow darted around the room as he lifted it. Several bottles lay broken and strewn on the floor of a makeshift dispensary divided from the sleeping quarters by a thin, dirty blanket. He held up the blanket with one hand and lifted the candle. He saw Gharoeb sitting upright, facing the corner. Moeraas called out in a half-whisper and on receiving no reply, advanced cautiously, allowing the blanket to fall gently.

'Gharoeb,' he called. There was no reply.

He touched the diviner's shoulder. Gharoeb keeled over and fell on his back. His face was ashen. His eyes had been gouged out.

DIE BUSHIE IS DOOD...

Johnny Jacobs lay bleeding in the road, his chestnut brown eyes widened in disbelief. He covered his face with his hands and shook his head. Life was ebbing out of him and he knew it.

'Why me? Why me, comrade Mandla? Why did they have to attack me of all people? Am I not also in the struggle?'

The words frothed from his mouth and he gripped on to the denim jacket of his best friend. The friend who had introduced him to student politics. It was 4.30 pm. The sun shone without real warmth for the June 16 rallyists who poured into the streets.

Johnny gave a rasping cough and spat out a mouthful of blood. The knives had sagged into him five times — in the back and on the chest. It happened without warning and Johnny's friends had scattered in all directions.

'Take me home, I want to die in my mother's house. Take me home comrade,' he said and began to cry. Mandla, who was equally baffled and angry at the attack on his friend, also cried. He put his hand on the injured boy's forehead.

'It's okay, Johnny. You are not going to die. It's okay my brother, I'm taking you home.'

How Mandla wished he could believe his own words. God, why did I bring him to Soweto? What will his family say? Remorse and anger burned inside him and brought more tears to his eyes. He lifted Johnny's head on to his lap. He looked up at the crowd whose numbers were increasing.

'Someone please call an ambulance! My friend is dying....' The words slipped out unintentionally. Mandla had fetched his comrade from Eldorado Park for the annual June 16 commemoration rally at Regina Mundi. He recollected

Johnny's fiery speech and his fervent call for greater unity and political and social interaction between the Coloureds, Indians and the African masses. Shouts of 'Viva! Viva!' had greeted his plea particularly at a time when many blacks were beginning to doubt the patriotism and loyalty of Coloureds and Indians to the broad, democratic struggle for liberation.

And now Johnny was dying.

When the comrade from Eldorado Park gasped for air, blood ran from the sides of his mouth and from the chest wounds. His yellow and red June 16 T-shirt with the historic Hector Pietersen emblem of sacrifice silkscreened on the front was drenched. The stain had begun to harden at the waist. An elderly man bent and loosened the belt, and remarked that the blood had wet Johnny's private parts. An irritated Mandla pushed the man's hands away.

'Who stabbed this Bushie?' enquired a deep baritone voice from the back of the crowd. Some people stared at the speaker wryly. 'It was the comrades from Dlamini,' volunteered a short, well-built girl dressed in a black skirt and yellow blouse — colours of the national student body which she supported. 'Three of them attacked the group that accompanied the coloured chap. They stabbed him several times,' she said in a conscious attempt to set the racial record straight. One only used the term 'maboesman' when Coloureds were at a safe distance. Discretion at times like these was vital, thought the girl, even though there were many Indians and Coloureds who spoke in a derogatory way about Blacks.

'I heard the poor guy scream,' said an apple and peanut vendor, pointing to the victim. 'He shouted: "Please don't kill me, I'm also a comrade." But they said: "Jy's 'n Bushie. You fokken Bushies don't want to strike and boycott when we strike and boycott." They were drunk. One of them returned and stabbed him one more time, and called him a sellout,' said the vendor. There was a loud murmur. Rumours abounded of imminent confrontation with the Coloureds and Indians over their apparent reluctance to join the strikes, stayaways and boycotts organised by the national movements. Comrade Mandla rose to his feet.

'Bushie or no Bushie, Johnny is one of us. He's black just like us and he's no bloody sellout. No sellout dammit!' Pain and anger were visible in his face.

Johnny recognised his voice. 'Take me home please,' he pleaded feebly. A woman dressed in the garb of a religious sect pushed through the crowd.

'Give him air,' she shouted. 'Give the boy air.' She removed a small blanket from around her waist, placed it under Johnny's head and stroked his curly brown hair. She did it gently, full of sympathy and concern. He could have been my own child, she thought.

'Give the poor boy air; move back,' she ordered again. She got up and pushed her way out.

The baritone voice came again: 'And what is he doing here, especially on a day like June 16? This is Soweto . . .' The jibe was cold and it clearly affected the bystanders. Many shook their heads while others nodded.

Soweto . . . Soweto . . . The word echoed in the injured boy's mind and trailed off into a soft but jagged sound: So . . . we . . . to . . . . The argument that morning in the yard: His mother's anger and her words 'I hope they kill you in that Soweto of yours . . .' drummed in his ears. Why did she have to curse me?

'Where the hell are you going to, Johnny? Why didn't you get up for college today?'

'It's June 16 ma, no teachers' college for me. I'm going to Soweto to attend a rally.'

'You're not going anywhere near that place. I'm sick of your bleddy politics. Those bantus are going to hurt you someday. If not the police then those people are going to give it to you; just wait and see. The last time you were picked up. Before that you were sjambokked at college; next time you will die, my boy.'

'Ma don't wish me bad luck and don't call them bantus. They are black people just like us.'

'Black, bantu, same bloody thing.' The speaker was Joe,

Johnny's eldest brother. 'Stay in your own area, among your own people and forget those darkies. They gonna necklace you for sure!'

Johnny shook his head. It was not the first time that his family had had it out with him. Members of the coloured community and its teaching fraternity had also attacked him for his political views. He swallowed the hastily made sandwich and bent in front of the watertap. The cold winter water pushed the bread down his gullet. He belched, wiped his mouth and took his newly bought June 16 T-shirt from a chair.

'Don't talk shit, Joe. Blacks don't just go around necklacing everybody. In fact it has stopped altogether. Besides it was used on police informers and sellouts.'

'Not just on sellouts, boetie. Those comrade friends of yours still use it to kill one another. The papers are full of such stories.'

Joe jumped up from the chair, grabbed the T-shirt and flung it into the dustbin.

'There. That's where that thing belongs — in the dirtbox.'

Johnny's fist slammed into his brother's face. Joe fell on his back. His mouth bled. He tried to rise but slumped backwards. Their mother screamed and flung a saucepan lid at her younger son as he retrieved the T-shirt. Johnny headed towards the gate where comrade Mandla and three friends waited in a green Dodge Colt.

'Don't come back here! I hope they kill you in that Soweto of yours. Bleddy politics. Will it never end?'

'I don't care!' responded her son as he entered the Dodge.

'What's wrong, Com? Is your old lady going crazy to curse you like that?'

'Naa, it's that stupid brother of mine. He threw this T-shirt in the dirtbox and I hit him hard.'

'Good. He's bloody mad. Your brother must be dagga drunk; that skipper is sacred to us blacks. Maybe not to coloureds but to us it is a symbol of great sacrifice.'

'Don't generalise, Com. Not all the coloureds are the same. And there are blacks among you who don't respect the significance of this Hector Pietersen T-Shirt. Behind your backs they sleep in the city and go to work on June 16. Not just the coloureds.'

'You are right. Put on your skipper, Soweto is calling us.'

'Soweto knows me. I've been attending June 16 rallies for the last seven years. When other kids in Eldorado go to college or school, I come to Soweto.'

'That's because you're a true comrade; one of us. What's more you've been detained, shot at and assaulted. You're one of the people, Com.'

'One of us, one of the people...' As Johnny whispered the words he gave a loud cough.

'What's he saying?' asked a tall bespectacled man, craning his head towards the victim.

'Something about people. I think the Bushie wants to be taken to his own people. I wonder what the hell he was doing here in the first place?' It was the deep baritone voice and what it said really irked Mandla.

'Shut up you fool; can't you see he's dying, dammit. Call the ambulance and stop talking shit. He's no bloody Bushie; he's black and he's my friend,' said Mandla and bit into his lip. Why, why did I bring him here?

Johnny lifted his head. 'Comrade take me home. I want to go to my mother's house.'

Mandla comforted him and put his head back on to the blanket. 'Rest comrade, rest...'

The ambulance arrived in the fading dusk. Its lights flickered dimly before Johnny's eyes.

'Stand back! Stand back!' shouted one of the attendants and pushed Mandla's hand from his friend's forehead. 'Come on,' came the authoritative command. 'Move away!'

'I'm with him. He's my friend. He's my brother,' said Mandla. Johnny smiled blankly. He coughed and jerked and kicked violently. The bleeding stopped. In fact there was no more blood in his body. One final cough. One final kick. One final question.

'Why me Com?'

The words were faint but Mandla heard them and cried uncontrollably. Johnny's eyes closed and his body released a great burst of air and then he lay still.

'He's gone,' said the deep baritone voice. 'Die Bushie is dood...'

DEATH CAN FOLLOW A MAN

The tall, almost leafless bluegum trees with their white bark winter overcoats were silent witnesses as the cold July wind whipped dry dust in Sarel Van Tonder's sad but stern face. There was a hard, belligerent anger in him as he stood granite-like — unmoved by the many handshakes of compassion and pity accompanied by kisses on his mouth and cheeks, and the soft pats on his back and shoulders. He needed nobody's compassion, let alone pity. When the farmhands began to fill the grave of his wife Annetta, Van Tonder moved away to rest his head against a barren and lifeless tree. Two forlorn shadows — a broken and distraught man, a gnarled and naked tree. As he closed his eyes he felt the grip of someone's strong hand on his arm. Xipu, the old Xhosa who had worked for the Van Tonder family, stared into his tear-filled eyes. The old man addressed him in Xhosa which Van Tonder understood and spoke fluently. A sudden, brief warmth showed in the white man's face and he nodded. This was one man whom he had loved and respected since childhood. A man whose compassion he could accept and trust. Xipu walked away without looking back.

A fierce, cold wind swept the leaves in all directions. The four raggedly-dressed coloured labourers bowed their heads as one of them recited the Lord's Prayer in broken Afrikaans. They looked so alike — even the two eighteen-year-olds among them appeared to be as aged as their older colleagues. Dejected quadruplets. Tattered, torn, dried out and covered from head to toe with the dust of a degradation visible only to the sensitive and perceptive observer.

Van Tonder had neither of these qualities.

Although he knew that his late wife had been especially fond of and kind to the coloured people, Van Tonder's suspicious eyes searched their faces to detect whether their sadness was genuine. 'Can't trust these hotnots,' he said to himself. 'They're good at acting. When they call a white man "baas" or "master", they're actually saying dog or pig.' His bitterness appeared to reach out to them and they simultaneously looked up at him.

'Maaster Sarel, sorry about the Klein Mies. She was always good to us,' said Bamboet the eldest. A coarse hand wiped his eyes. Bamboet's brand of Afrikaans was unlike that of the white people. Van Tonder understood but remained impassive. The quadruplets walked to the farther side of the cemetery. They climbed through a hole in the fence and headed towards the valley where their sombre, grey shacks waited for them. Lovers at the homecoming. Van Tonder watched their departure through the corner of his eye. Why could I not bring myself to like or trust these people? Why did I go out of my way to humiliate them? I must learn to change my ways.

In that state of temporary contrition, he moved towards the grave. A cold shiver, aggravated by a choking lump in the throat, overcame him. He bent and placed his bony hand on the hump of sand. The smell of the remaining bluegum leaves and the scent of the asters sank into him like needles. The shivering worsened. Tears rolled on to his hand. He flung the Bible into the dead grass.

'Gott, Annetta,' he screamed. 'Why did you have to die? It was all so needless. So unnecessary, so futile!'

The man was now beside himself with sorrow, whimpering like a child afraid of the dark. Afraid of life. Afraid of the days ahead without his beloved Annetta. And what of the child she had left behind — a child he had not wanted for fear that she would die as those damned doctors had warned. Recollecting that warning compounded his sorrow and anger.

Sorrow and anger. How they can rip the heart apart and cut away the flesh, and break the bone and burn the spirit with a desire to end life . . . .

Van Tonder, still shouting madly, grabbed the wreaths and

the flowers and flung them at the people who had come to pay their last respects. Some of the men pinned him down. A woman began weeping hysterically. Another shouted: 'Hy's mal. Die arme man is gek!' Her words jolted him into composure. The strong grips on him relaxed. He was left lying face-down on the grave, sobbing. The mourners left and headed towards the Van Tonder house for tea and other refreshments as was the custom after a burial.

Inside the house, Ester Pietersen, the buxom and softly-spoken domestic worker, cuddled the three-week-old baby boy. Annetta had eagerly wanted a son in order to perpetuate the Van Tonder family name. A son would be her best gift to the man she passionately loved. A man who in turn had worshipped and loved her despite her physical deformity. Ester fondled the baby tenderly in the same manner she had cared for its mother not so many years before. The past three weeks had been most trying for Ester. Her employer had hardened towards the child to the point of even refusing to hold or look at it. 'Take him away. I hate him. Through that damned child's birth my beautiful Annetta lost her life. Take him away from me,' Van Tonder had shouted when Ester asked him to hold the child. That was on the night before the funeral — two days after her death. Nothing had changed. Her fears for the child's safety increased when she heard the mourners recount the incident at the graveside.

'So help my Gott, ek sal hom doodmaak as hy die keend touch,' she said aloud and pressed her round cheeks against Klein Sarel's face. There could be no doubt, she would kill him.

The cemetery now lay far behind as Van Tonder ascended the austere Graaff Reinet mountain range, almost tripping over the shiny stones and the darting lizards. He had deliberately avoided using the familiar and traditional pathway, for fear of being seen and stopped from doing the thing he had set his mind on. On the eastern side of the slopes lay the African village with its whitewashed matchbox dwellings. He had loved the area as a child when Xipu used to bring him to meet the Xhosa people. It was there that he had learned to speak their language. There that he had sex with a black girl for the first time. It seemed like only yesterday.

He spat and watched the warm sand suck the spit just as it would suck and cover him. Annetta! The thought of her name brought back the memory of their chance meeting on the verandah of Smit's Grocery Store in Graaff Reinet. She was carrying a heavy bag and had limped badly on a clubbed foot. Sweat gave a beautiful lustre to her face, highlighting the black tresses which hung loosely on her small shoulders. Annetta had bumped into Van Tonder and they landed on the ground. A Xhosa woman had laughed hysterically and shouted for all to hear: 'Aaii bantu! It is true when they say the big toes are blind! Just look there, they don't see where they are walking. Just look!'

They got up and shared the joke — laughing as they had not laughed in many years. She lived in the tiny town of Pearston, situated between Graaff Reinet and Janssenville in the Eastern Cape Province. After that meeting, he had visited her regularly. Then came the wedding and two good years of wedded bliss. Then came that bloody child and Annetta's useless death. Sorrow and anger welled up in him anew and he bit his lip and clenched his fists. It must end. It *will* end....

The plunge would be swift and final. Van Tonder looked at the rocks below. Two brown-and-gold lizards with black spots on their backs and legs frolicked amorously as they prepared to make love. The winter sun glistened on their bodies and they ran over his black shoes, catching his eye. The distraction was brief. 'It will end now. Annetta, my Annetta, I'm coming,' he said aloud. Xipu who had been sharpening his knife on a stone to cut the biltong in his pocket, looked up from behind a huge rock. He saw the lanky, wiry Van Tonder trembling and sobbing uncontrollably.

'Aauw Tixo wam,' he shouted. 'Don't jump. Please, my son, don't jump.' In that brief moment that Van Tonder turned his face, Xipu grabbed him round the waist, locking both arms in a vice-like grip. 'No, my son, this is not the way. Your life is too precious.' The resistance in the white man's body collapsed. The steel grip had weakened him just as the three weeks of pining and anger had done. Xipu felt the resignation but would not let go. 'By my ancestors, this bird will not fly.' He moved away from the precipice, half-dragging his charge. Van Tonder spoke quietly in the language of the old man. 'I am fine now, Tata. You can leave me alone. I am composed. Twice you have rescued me. Once as a child you pulled me from the burning house which took my parents, my brothers and sisters. And now again.' Xipu loosened his grip and nodded. The men parted ways at the foot of the sullen and imposing mountains. Xipu who genuinely loved and cared for Van Tonder, watched the distraught man vanish behind a cluster of farmhouses.

Ester too watched her employer's every move as he violently pushed the door ajar and strutted into the corridor towards the pinewood staircase which led to the spacious bedrooms.

Annetta had adorned the baby's adjoining room with attractive wallpaper and ornaments. Ester too, had been like a hen, fretting and fidgeting around her sickly 'miesies', to the open irritation of Van Tonder. 'Donderse teef,' she had heard him say once. Being called a bitch would not change or diminish her love and loyalty for Annetta whose mother Kristina she had also raised and cared for.

As Van Tonder placed his foot on the third step, he stared at the huge photograph on the wall — their wedding picture. He called his wife's name several times, raising his voice. Ester appeared. 'Het maaster geroep?' Their gaze met. Her eyes widened at the pitiful spectacle he had become — his cold eyes were filled with so much pain and aloneness. Van Tonder descended, took the photograph from the wall. He sat on the steps and stared at Ester.

'Gott vroumens, can't a man cry without you poking your fat face in my sorrow? Must you always stare at me like that?'

'But I heard a noise and thought....'

'You thought shit. I didn't kill her. I loved her more than life itself. Can you understand that?' His words were compelling and cold.

'I know that maaster loved my Annetta.' There was compassion in her tone. He detected it and flung more vitriol at her. 'That child, that bloody little killer, he murdered her....'

The frame fell at his feet. The glass shattered and awakened the child. Ester ran past him. 'Here,' she exclaimed invoking God's name, 'die man het sy senses verloor. Hy's regtig mal.' She lifted Klein Sarel from the cot and pacified him. Van Tonder bent down to retrieve the photograph. His tears soaked into a small carpet at the foot of the staircase. He slowly climbed the steps to his bedroom. He opened his liquor cabinet, took out a bottle of brandy — something he had not done during the happy two years of his marriage. He flung the cap towards the open door and swallowed several times.

He gasped for breath, taking in all the air his lungs could carry. The bottle fell from his hand and its contents spilled on to the wooden flooring, emitting a rich strong odour. Wind entered through the open windows and the curtains danced to their own choreography and hit against an empty vase which fell and smashed into pieces. The child cried. Ester again took him from his cot and ascended the steps. She peeped into the bedroom and saw Van Tonder's head buried in the pillows. His body shook violently. She made her way down to the kitchen and placed her charge in his cot. She cleaned the big pile of cups, saucers, plates and wine glasses.

How Van Tonder's neighbours and the mourners had eaten and gossiped about his unbecoming screaming and wailing at Annetta's grave. One woman, Dominee Koot Swanepoel's wife, had whispered to her friend Johanna Jansson: 'Mark my words suster Johanna, Sarel won't even wait one month and another woman will jump into his bed. All the men are the same

— they don't even wait for your bed to get cold. Mark my words.'

'All the same, Trina,' agreed her friend. 'and did you see the show he put up at the cemetery? What hypocrisy, and all that in front of those hotnots and natives. Imagine!'

Ester mused over the word 'hotnots'. 'Sies,' she said aloud. 'Die bleddie goed het so gevreet en gedrink. Al my maaster se bleddie wyn!' Their gossiping reminded her of the time she had worked for Annetta's parents. Joost du Plooy, the dead girl's father, killed himself following his arrest — and that of a black woman — on charges under the dreaded Immorality Act. Du Plooy had worked as a foreman at a farm in Janssenville not far from Kristina's hometown, Pearston. Recollecting the sordid events made Ester shudder. The news and the gossiping, wagging tongues of the white women had really shocked her at the time. Heaven forbid that it should ever happen again.

Her thoughts were stirred by the soft crying of the child. She lifted him into her arms and sang a lullaby which she had sung as a young girl. A lullaby that told of a summer breeze that always caressed the boughs of a willow tree it loved. The rhythm was gentle. Her body swayed to and fro until the child fell asleep again. Upstairs, Van Tonder slept soundly. The huge drapes continued their dance routine to the music of the wind. Ester's mind reached back as the reel of memory re-screened the events which had led to Du Plooy's and his wife's destruction. Kristina was pregnant at the time and resting on a couch in the sitting-room when a policeman called on her. Ester was asked to leave the room but she heard the conversation from outside the door.

'Why was my husband arrested, Captain? What did he do — kill someone?'

'Worse than that, Mevrou Du Plooy.'

'What could be worse, Captain?'

'Well he was found in bed with a black woman!'

'A black woman? O my Gott; my goeie Gott. A black woman!'

She got up, then slumped to the floor. The policeman called out to Ester. They placed Kristina on her bed. The captain ordered Ester to tell her 'miesies' that bail had been fixed at fifty pounds. He felt sorry for the woman he had hurt with the disturbing and unholy news. For there was no crime among the Afrikaners quite like that of having sex with a black man or a black woman. It was the Eleventh Commandment: 'Thou shall not make love to a black person.' Black and white together? No. Never the twain to meet except as master and servant; 'miesies' and 'meid'; 'baas' and 'boy'.

This was the law. And Ester knew and feared this unwritten commandment.

In all her years as a 'meid', she knew that this was one law she should never transgress. Crockery she could break and be forgiven for but sleeping with a white man was unpardonable. A great, dark sin against the Volk and God. God forgave, but not the Volk.

'Worse than murder,' the police captain had said.

Ester's childhood days in the factoryless Pearston stirred from the cradle of her mind. She could see herself walking hand-in-hand with her father Toon Pietersen to the farm school across the dry countryside in Janssenville. He was a strong man who worked as a Jack-of-all-trades to maintain his family of six boys and four girls. Most of Pearston's black and white inhabitants respected Toon and the coloured people relied on his leadership. He excelled as a rugby player and tinsmith. There wasn't a shack or home in Graaff Reinet, Pearston and Janssenville that didn't have one of Toon's products — baths, dishes, washbasins and sieves.

As the lastborn child, Ester was spoilt by her father. He once took her to Cape Town to buy her a white dress with matching socks, ribbons and shoes for the 'aanneming' ceremony — her acceptance into the Kerk, rather the coloured wing of the Kerk. For to live and pray together was not in keeping with the law of the Volk. In worship, as in social and cultural life, never the twain to meet. It was a long journey and she had slept on her father's lap. It was from him also that she had learned the lullaby about the summer breeze and the willow tree.

When the Second World War broke out, Toon and other coloured men enlisted. He was sent to North Africa with a large contingent of African soldiers but their ship was bombarded. There was no burial place for Toon except the bluegum tree — the bloekomboom which Ester had planted near a tiny range of hillocks outside Pearston. It became a place of pilgrimage for the man she loved. Her mother died after the great turning-point election which saw the Afrikaners rise to power and inculcate into their people a sense of superiority and arrogance. Yet there were many of the Boers who retained their humanity and dealt fairly with the indigenous folk. Kristina's parents — the Timmermans — were among them. Humane and compassionate.

Kristina was an only child, and after her marriage to Du Plooy, her parents moved to Cape Town and lived and died on their vineyards. Ester had been hired to work for Kristina. So much water had flowed under Ester's bridge since those days. She had never really found someone to love although Martiens, the son of Herman Swartz the farm school principal, had seduced her on the pretext that he would marry her. But the young handsome seducer fled to Port Elizabeth and she had never heard of him again. Ester gave a long, deep sigh and slumped into a chair. It all seemed just like yesterday. How she missed her father.

Ester had always known about Du Plooy's sexual escapades with black women. 'Boere-sport' the young and old Afrikaner bulls used to call their 'games' of sleeping with black women in the dark roads and alleys. Yet, thought Ester, what sorcery did the black body hold for white men and their womenfolk? Ester felt a warmth in her body just thinking about it. What fire burns in the loins of white men when they look at us? Du Plooy had once tried it on her when Kristina was away shopping in the city. His right hand had reached under her dress and his left hand around her throat. His hot breath burned against her neck and his chest heaved almost to bursting point. Du Plooy's fingers penetrated her — searching and feeling. How she wanted to surrender to his hunger and his strength. How. As if remembering the Eleventh Commandment, he had violently pushed her against the wall and said: 'Teef, say one word and you're dead. One bloody word . . . .'

A wicked smile crossed her face. The thought of her near-submission brought fire to her body. It was years since she last slept with a man. She had been attracted to Du Plooy in a way she had not comprehended. Kristina too was deeply in love with him and had taken money to bail him out. On that day she had driven their car like a woman possessed — hardly breathing properly. She allowed her tears to flow freely. The money in her hand was moist from the sweat of shame and pain and humiliation that tugged at her heart.

It was towards evening. The car had sped along the sand road, raising a massive dustcloud behind it. Her foot pressed hard on the accelerator. Faster. Faster. Like the thoughts inside her mind. She bit deep into her lip. What would the people say? How would she be able to live with the shame of it all — a fate and crime worse than murder? Faster. The sweat of anxiety rolled into her eyes. Faster. She raced against her thoughts. Against her fears. Against the humiliation that would follow her for the rest of her life. Her foot was now flat against the accelerator. She felt a knot in her stomach — in the pit of her soul where all the dark sin and shame breeds and lays its eggs. She gasped for air and lost control. The car spun several times and crashed into a tree. Some farmhands found her the next morning badly injured but alive — the bail money still tightly gripped in her bloodied fist. Her teeth had locked on to her tongue.

When the news reached Du Plooy at the police station, he reeled backwards against the cell wall, stunned.

'Do you see what your sinning and lust have brought on your

family — nothing but tragedy and punishment.' The indictment came from the police captain who had informed Kristina of the crime worse than murder. 'Remember that when you mount the next black teef, Du Plooy,' said the captain.

The perpetrator of the 'grievous crime' nodded his admission of sin and guilt. The Volk would not be mocked. God and forgiveness had nothing to do with it. All that mattered now was retribution and penance. They found him the next morning hanging from the rafters of his cell — his belt firmly tied around his neck. The Volk had been paid in full.

The slate had been cleaned.

Kristina who gave birth two nights after the accident, never fully recovered from her injuries. She was committed to a mental home where she died. A neighbour of the Timmermans, Anna Scheepers, had adopted the child Annetta whom Ester raised and cared for through school and marriage. Her clubbed foot was a direct result of the crash. But Annetta too was now gone. Ester cried at the thought of the tragedies that had befallen the Du Plooys.

And what of the man called Van Tonder who had become utterly irrational because of sorrow and heartbreak? Could the distraught creature be blamed for holding Annetta's death against their baby? What would the future bring? Ester felt compassion for her employer and climbed the stairs to check on him. The bed was empty. She picked up the broken vase, closed the windows and placed the brandy bottle on a small table near the bed. Back in the kitchen her charge slept soundly. The wintry night brought a quiet peace to the house.

When the sun rose over Gaaf — as the Xhosa and coloured people have named Graaff Reinet — its red, yellow and orange rays reached down to touch the tips of the black hillocks and the huge mountains which appeared to carry the morning sheen on their shoulders. Then down towards the sparse grasslands to where the sheep and the goats would later graze, the sunlight poured its blessing. People stirred inside the single-row shacks and smoke curled from the makeshift chimneys. The smell of burning wood rose up and filled the nostrils of the sky.

Life came to Gaaf without the blood-pumping madness of a big industrialised city. The liquid sunrays dripped stealthily through the myriad holes in the zinc roof of Xipu's dwelling. When he opened the door, a bright burst of light fell on his chocolate brown face.

'Tixo wam,' he exclaimed, partly cursing and partly grateful for the gift of experiencing another day. He took water from a clay pot and rinsed his mouth. A few drops rolled over his face. He thought of the journey ahead to Pearston where he had been offered a job on Du Toit's farm. The walk would be a long one and he decided that he would have to cut across the mountain range. Xipu broke off a piece of stale bread and wrapped the remainder in an old newspaper. He chewed slowly and turned the key to lock the door — rattling the knob several times to ensure that it was indeed locked. Satisfied, he made his way towards the mountains, choosing as always, the familiar footpath.

Xipu was not one to walk the main roads. Not for him lifts and pity. His Tixo who ruled the mountains and sent the rain when it pleased him — this Tixo had given him sturdy legs to carry his ageing body on the long road of life. And now in his old age, his legs would not fail him. His grandfather and uncles had always told him that only a strong tree trunk could hold many branches and carry much fruit. For his age, Xipu walked fast. He left the commonly-used footpath to cut across a small hill. He reached for his small knife and for the biltong in the leather pouch. He cut off a piece and began chewing. Saliva gathered on the sides of his mouth. As he approached a cleft which led to the top of his favourite mountain, Xipu tripped and fell on his back. Stunned and in pain, he lay still and looked up at the sky. Several minutes passed. Out of breath and somewhat disappointed with himself, Xipu got up and sat on a rock. He retraced his tracks but saw nothing which could have caused him to fall.

'Tixo wam. I have walked these paths so many times that I could reach the top blindfolded. Yet what could have gone wrong?' he asked himself aloud. Perhaps it was the end of the road for him? He had never before thought of death. Yet how would it come for him? In his sleep or on these beloved mountains? Xipu shook his head and clicked his tongue. Who knows the hour or the place or the day? And although he had no living relatives that he could think of, Xipu felt certain that his people, the amaXhosa, would bury him. They had many failings and shortcomings, but in the matter of death and burial — and of adhering to traditions and customs — they were reliable. How life was changing. Old age and death, how inseparable and inevitable they were. He jerked himself to his feet in an attempt to convince himself that he was still fit to continue his journey into the remaining years. He turned his head for a last look at the path which had in such a short moment reminded him of his frailty and vulnerability. His eyes scanned the footpath. He clicked his tongue. 'Tixo,' he exclaimed when he saw Van Tonder's lifeless hand reaching out from among the dry shrubs.

The fall from the top had been swift.

Xipu shook his head and sank to the ground. He held the cold hand in his palms and then to his face. 'Aauw Tixo, Tixo wam. Death, how it can follow a man.'

Inside the house Ester sang a lullaby to Annetta's baby and rubbed her round cheeks against its soft, pink skin.

THE STORYTELLER

There is a mountain range near Kammagas in the north-western Cape region of our beautiful and bewitching country, South Africa, which appears to shield a valley and its inhabitants from the forceful winds that circle and rise beyond the range. In a split between the rocks there is a footpath that snakes crookedly to vanish into a cluster of mud-and-wood shacks below. The shacks have makeshift thatch and rusty tin roofs secured with huge stones against the might of the winds. That village is called Gamka. It was the home of about five hundred farm labourers and herdsmen — women, men and children — who worked for the white sheep and goat farmers of Kammagas. No black person was allowed to stay in Kammagas; only to shed their labour and then to migrate after sunset to their nook between the mountains.

It was the law and the eighth year of National Party rule since the fateful election of 1948.

Gaap Slingers, a shepherd of many long years, was the oldest and perhaps the wisest citizen of Gamka, or so the people believed and Gaap was not one to argue against them. Besides the traditional respect and deference with which his people treated him, there were gifts of snuff, old clothes and dresses for his twin grand nieces. Silbermann, the Jewish auctioneer whose bags he had carried to the motel at Kammagas, gave him an old black-and-white oversized tailcoat and a bow tie. Short, stocky and muscular, Gaap was loved by the children of the village for his gentleness and his ability to tell interesting stories about everything under God's sun. Plants, people and animals; stories about the olden days; about the great wars between the tribes, and the battles against the early colonial settlers. Gaap was a source of strength and inspiration to his people. Respected. Loved.

The mountains knew him as they did the wind and the dust that beat against their stony brows. And the heat and the cold, when they came in their seasons, first touched the mountains with respect before heading down to the village.

Gaap was a frequent visitor to the mountains where, with searing words, he would speak to his Creator in the language of his Khoisan forebears of the things that pleased or troubled his heart and spirit. Many people came to Gaap for advice and remedies for their ailing children and themselves. There was no illness he could not cure with his vast knowledge of traditional herbal medicines — or so the simple folk believed, and through their faith, they were made whole. They all came to him — the rich and the poor; white and black. Gaap had no-one to turn to when his heart was burdened or when the twins cried and pined after their mother. To the mountains, always to them to speak and pray and to find solace. The diminutive shepherd was among the last of the oral poets of his people. He was also a storyteller and teacher and many spoke of his strength and gentleness which made him appear younger than his actual seventy-two years. Gaap had a compelling magnetism in his narrow eyes which attracted the noisy and inquisitive children to his side. Even the children of the Boers and those of the few Jewish and English-speaking whites came to him to hear some of the history they did not learn at their schools.

'Tell us stories,' the children of Gamka called out to him. They touched and held his hands and led him to their favourite spot. The storyteller always followed them meekly; no longer a shepherd but one of the flock. It was a role he loved and he smiled warmly when the children placed him on the flat stone which had become his traditional storytelling seat.

'Oom Gaap, tell us about our ancestors who lived and roamed this part of the earth long before the blacks and white tribes came. Tell us about the mountains and valleys our forebears inhabited, and of the animals and insects whose language our people understood. Tell us of the wars they fought and lost and how the land was taken from them.'

The shepherd chuckled loudly. His eyes narrowed further for it was his best-loved topic; one which he narrated with the art and hidden psychology of his forebears. It gave him a sense of pride and authority to be able to recount the tales of the San and the Khoikhoi. As far as he was concerned, no-one could challenge or dispute his facts. And why would they when everything that he told them was in their favour. Even the educated 'meesters' — the teachers, called on him to learn more about the old ways and what life was like in the places the white man calls Bushmanland and Namakwaland. The schoolteachers also wanted to hear about the place called Namib to which many of the San and Khoikhoi fled following attacks by the 'Jackals' who came from across the great foamy waters. It was a long time ago, but the history had been carried down to Gaap in the oral tradition; somewhat exaggerated but carried down nonetheless.

And the children listened wide-eyed and with open mouths to the tales of the San and the Khoikhoi, the Chocoqua and the Kwena-Kwena, and the many sub-tribes who inhabited South Africa from the South of and across the Orange River. That was long before the other indigenous tribes of Africa had occupied the areas west of the Orange. Many of these tribes settled near the Vaal River where they established trade or bartering stations.

The Khoisan tribes set up communities on the shores of the Western Cape sea routes from what has become known as Walvis Bay, into the Kalaghari, Bechuanaland and across to the Eastern Cape, and past East Griekwaland where Adam Kok had his kingdom, and whose horsemen were feared and respected in battle. Men who joined the Barolong, and the other black tribes as well as the Voortrekkers, in the great battle against Mzilikazi. Then from Griekwaland, the Khoisan trekked to what the English called Richards Bay and then inland to the north of Natal; as far as the eye could see above the Valley of a Thousand Hills. Then past the ominous Drakensberg mountain range where the white dragons lived, and then down to the great rivers that swell from the foamy waters which fall suicidally from the high rocks. All that was the domain of the Khoisan peoples. There they lived and ended their days without want or hindrance. Gaap's voice fell to a whisper.

He told the children of the tall and powerful tribes of the Nguni who had descended from across the great and small plains. Some of them travelled through the Horn of Africa in the East.

'They came to the vast, green valleys and grasslands and settled to begin a dominion that drove the Khoisan from the area. The Nguni were brave warriors who planned their battles with military precision that bewildered the Khoisan. The strong heads and long spears of the Nguni appeared to touch the sky. Tall, majestic and fearless, they towered above the Khoisan warriors,' said the Storyteller, 'and became known as the "Nation of the Heavens" — amaZulu. Although the Khoisan were defeated, many Nguni soldiers died from the sting of poisoned arrows. Then began the long exodus through the heartland where the Basotho and Pedi tribes lived. But finding no hospitality there, the Khoisan found refuge and generosity among the Barolong with whom they intermarried and lived and shared and exchanged cultures, customs and tradition.'

The narrative continued: 'The Nguni tribe split into several units: Zulu, Xhosa, Swazi and Ndebele. After many years of peaceful co-existence, wars erupted between Mzilikazi's Ndebeles and the other tribes — the Basotho, Pedi and the Barolong. As a result thousands of Khoisan and their assimilated Barolong women and Barolong sons-in-law headed back to the Western Cape where the main body of their kinsfolk had their domain. Other tribes like the Mbanderu, the Namas and the Ghoranas, settled in the Kalaghari.'

'The amaXhosa moved to the Eastern Cape where they established kingdoms on both banks of the Great Kei River. They also split into several sub-units of which the Tembus, were the strategists and thinkers. Years later, after the Great Battle between the Khoikhoi nation and the "Jackals", hundreds of Khoi families sought and were given refuge among the amaXhosa, particularly among the Fingos who assimilated them, resulting in a cultural and linguistic fusion which influenced both the language and the traditions of both peoples.'

The Gamka children listened in silence to that history, nodding as their shepherd recounted the past, gesticulated with his strong hands and feet and made marks and drawings in the sand. Gaap held them enthralled. He spun a web of magic and occult bewilderment; a master of the Oral Tradition. He told them of the great sickness — 'die pes' — the pestilence which attacked the body with many little sores that left holes in the face. Thousands of Khoisan perished from the disease which had also weakened their nation in other battles against the foreigners whose hair hung below their shoulders — like the tails of the jackals.

Gaap stared at them, contented that his tales had sunk into their hearts and minds. He got up to gather more firewood and dry shrubs which he neatly piled onto the embers. He bent down and huffed and puffed at the coals until the flames rose high; yellow and orange and apricot like the skins of his ancestors. The flames leaped higher and danced to their own music; magical and mystifying. The children's eyes followed the darting sparks on the short journeys into space. Xai-Xai, the eldest boy in the group and also the most inquisitive, cleared his throat loudly to draw their attention. They picked up the cue and looked deferentially at their leader.

'Taa-Gaap,' said Xai-Xai, using a term of endearment. 'Tell them more about the Jackals who took our land.' The boy's chest swelled to twice its normal size. Full and bursting with pride. His eyes scanned the faces of his impressionable followers. Some of them shared in his pride while others feared him. Xai-Xai moved with authority among them and had fought and won several fist fights against the children of the white farmers. He was a fighter and the children of Gamka accepted his leadership without question. No-one really knew his origin. In fact he was found in the bushes by Karatua during a cold winter's night. She had been on her way back to Gamka after exorcising evil spirits at the home of the superstitious Kees Wilkens the hide tanner and mat manufacturer who lived outside the town of Kammagas. Karatua also sold herbs and roots to a Cape Town naturopath and had been counting her money when the loud wailing of Xai-Xai shocked her and caused her to stumble. She took him to her home and raised him. When her daughters married and left the village, Xai-Xai the faithful, as he came to be known, took the responsibility of caring for Karatua.

The boy was intelligent and attended school at the Concordia Lutheran Mission two miles from Gamka. It was during the history lessons that he asked irritating questions about the land and the people who had inhabited it before the whites came. He completed the eighth standard but left school to work and care for his ageing foster mother who was a close friend of Gaap Slingers. Xai-Xai often eavesdropped when the old couple met on the rare occasions that the shepherd visited Karatua. He especially liked to listen to the bursts of laughter which always ended with his foster mother coughing hoarsely from the dagga which she smoked and used as medicine. She became addicted to smoking it after a bout of illness.

'Taa-Gaap,' persisted the bright Xai-Xai, 'some of these boys come from Pofadder. They say that although their villages have storytellers like you, they have not heard this history.' There was a note of pleading in the boy's voice — an urgency, and the shepherd knew he could not refuse, especially as the other children had grown to respect the talkative Xai-Xai. Gaap looked at the boy and smiled. He saw part of himself in the alert and sensitive eyes. The same pride and confidence and fire that he had felt as a young man. Xai-Xai could read and write — feats which he, Gaap, had not learned for all his years on earth. The lad had the makings of a leader who would stand his ground and take his place among men. Of this, Gaap was certain. He knew it was more than ordinary curiosity that had urged Xai-Xai to ask him to relate the story about the coming of the white man. Lies had been written and told about the San and the Khoikhoi — the so-called Bushmen and Hottentots who were said to be lazy, uncivilised and unproductive thieves.

Before his mentor could speak, Xai-Xai said: 'Taa-Gaap says they call our people Hotnots and Boesmans. What is a Hottentot? There was no tribe in Africa by that name, according to our elders. The white people say we worshipped a beetle called "Hotnotsgod".' His voice trailed to a whisper. Gaap's response and support convinced the boy of the correctness of his cause and the fallacy of the history written and propagated by the white historians. In fact the boy had only repeated what he had heard from Gaap.

'It is all lies, my son. Our God was and is the One whom the Xhosas call Tixo. It is our name for the Creator who rules the earth, the sky and all things living and dead. Hotnotsgod was only one of the many insults that the Khoikhoi and the San have had to endure.'

And Xai-Xai knew what Gaap had known as a young man: their history had been demeaned in the same way that they as a people were humiliated. Their history was a proud one of art and culture — beset with the same problems of good and evil; success and failure; crime and punishment. For although men spoke derogatorily about them as 'Boesmans and Hotties', he, Gaap, knew that they were Africans. And no-one could take that away from them; no matter what.

The boy smiled as the saga unfolded. 'Yes,' said the shepherd, 'they came from across the raging waters in huge ships whose white sails fluttered in the wind. Our people, who had seen many of those ships through the angry, stormy waters, ululated and sang when the Jackals brought their vessels to a halt. Our womenfolk even helped to unload and carry the cargo inland to safer and higher ground. We made fires and gave them fresh meat and milk and corn and potatoes. They smoked our weed and took the snuff we had offered. We in turn, received their gifts of beads, cloth and wine with the same openness with which the Jackals gave them to us. All was at peace.'

Gaap told the children of the long rifles that made the cattle fall to their knees from a distance. There were no women among the strangers and many Khoikhoi and San maidens shared their bodies with the men from across the sea. Their children lived among our people. For many years more ships arrived and brought with them more men. It was not long and the Jackals manned several outposts in the land of the Khoikhoi and created camps for the rebellious slaves they brought into the Cape. Their slaves came from colonies usurped by the Jackals following the subjugation of the native peoples, the children were told.

The shepherd chose his words carefully and deliberately; placing the appropriate and emotive emphasis on certain key phrases with the skillful mastery needed to maximise the effect on the minds of his audience. The fire was dying but for a few embers. Gaap motioned to Xai-Xai to get more wood. And before long huge flames pointed their yellow tongues at the sky as if to direct the gazes of the young listeners to the birth and beauty of the myriad stars which pierced the blanket of night with their sharp light. But no, their gazes remained fixed on the old man.

Gaap stopped speaking for a while. He placed snuff on the back of his hand. His head sank forward and he inhaled the snuff. The children watched every move and marvelled at the dexterity with which the ritual was performed. The narrative was resumed: 'After a few years of peace the Jackals, whose numbers had increased dramatically, ordered our people into camps alongside the slaves they had brought into the land; slaves who spoke many different languages and sang wailing and plaintive songs.'

Xai-Xai got up and asked if he could speak. Gaap nodded. The boy smiled: 'Yes, the Jackals taught our people about a new god but many of our ancestors rejected their religion. They told the Jackals that the God of the Khoikhoi and the San was united with his creation in all things. He was one with the earth, the sky and with nature; God of the mountains and the rivers, the grass and the shrubs, the trees and one with all the beasts and insects that lived on the earth. And, and ... well everything. Isn't it so, Taa-Gaap?' He turned to his mentor for approval and Gaap nodded slowly.

Xai-Xai smiled broadly and continued: 'The elders tell us that our ancestors had rejected the interpretation which the Jackals gave to the One Almighty Creator. But it was not long and many of our people adopted the faith and ways of the Jackals. The people were given salt, tobacco, dried meat and wine, and those kinds of things. Their collars were removed and they were given land and declared free men.' The boy shook his head several times and laughed aloud. 'First their land was taken and they were put into chains. Then when they accepted the new God of the Jackals and the man they claimed was his son, they were fed, freed and given a piece of their own land.' Xai-Xai threw up his hands in frustration, causing brief laughter from his captive audience.

Gaap nodded. The wrinkles deepened when he frowned. There was a degree of wisdom in the boy which he could not fathom. It was more than just plain rebelliousness but something deeper. There were times when he and Xai-Xai would go walking and talking about life and death and the many complexities that transcend scrutiny; things of the spirit which a boy or girl his age would dismiss as nonsense. But this Xai-Xai, this querulous and restless child, displayed the traits of great leadership and courage. If there was going to be one to lead their people, then it would surely be him. He is a great orator. Gaap's thoughts raced faster when he felt Xai-Xai's grip against his arm. Both mentor and pupil smiled broadly.

The shepherd took up the story again: 'What Xai says is true. Those of our people who refused to be pressed down took up arms. A bloody battle ensued. The rifles of the Jackals roared many times. Our warriors fell. The holes in their chests were huge and deep. Blood flowed thick and red and stained the rocks and the sand. Hundreds upon hundreds of men and women fell. Some never to rise again. Those who did get up never looked back as they fled. Those who could not flee were captured and bound against the trees.

'And the women were taken. And the land that was ours became the property of the Jackals whose offspring control it to this day.' The old man sighed deeply.

Some of the children nodded not fully comprehending the depth of their storyteller's words. And in those moments of silence they soaked in every syllable, every nuance and gesture that Gaap had made. Surely there was no-one in the land who could tell stories like their shepherd. Of that they were certain. Gaap's right thumb and index finger again pinched deep into the sheepskin pouch and placed snuff on the back of his strong hands where the veins stood up like small railway lines. That way no-one would suspect that he had actually been crying. No-one except the alert and sensitive Xai who always scrutinised his face, and took in every word and action that he, Gaap, made.

Surely if there was to be a leader for the people, then it would be his Xai-Xai.

The children scanned the storyteller's face without saying a word. They had heard the tale before but on each occasion it expanded beyond their wildest dreams; unfolding rich and full of realism. Then one by one they got up and went their different ways until only Gaap and Xai-Xai remained. They sat in silence trying to read each other's thoughts; quietly triumphant in their conspiracy. Xai, unlike many of the labourers, had refused to forsake the sanctity of the old customs and culture of the Khoisan.

When that was lost, all would be lost, Gaap had once told him.

The old man spoke: 'I am happy that you among so many of our people still revere and hold dear the old ways. Although everything is changing around us, we must recognise and acknowledge the good that comes to our people and to the land. But we must not deny our roots and traditions. They are all we have left, my son.'

Xai-Xai nodded. The old man continued: 'The old ways are

dying. Tradition too is dying in Gamka and in the places where the blacks live. Someday young men and women like you will emerge to lead our people back to their dignity and manhood.' Gaap's words shot through the boy like a scorpion's sting so that his skin crawled. Xai-Xai again nodded several times and got up to embrace his mentor.

Someday he would lead his people to freedom.

The old man too was emotionally touched. He bit his teeth hard; teeth which he brushed regularly with the root of a mountain shrub. They were strong and clean. His oval face was defined and the high cheekbones had a lustre unlike that of people his age.

Gaap lived with his niece's twin daughters Griet and Toekies, whose mother Talaah was the only child of his late sister Manga. Talaah had run away from their home with a 'Joster' — a man from Johannesburg — when the twins were barely one year old.

Restlessness and a taste for adventure had driven Talaah into the Joster's arms and finally into his heart. It all began when his car stopped alongside the road leading towards the white town.

'Verskoon my dame, hoe kom 'n mens uit na Kammagas?' he said asking the way to the white town. Talaah smiled at being called a lady; something she was unaccustomed to because her people were referred to as 'outah' and 'meid'. This man, this terribly handsome stranger who had called her lady in pure Afrikaans, had a skin as apricot-coloured as hers.

'Gits,' said Talaah, using a colloquialism. She pointed towards the neat rows of trees. 'There's only white people staying there you know.'

He smiled and offered her a lift. He put the pile of firewood in the boot of his car. The vehicle rolled gently over the sand. As she alighted, Talaah's eyes searched the Joster's face. A sensual smile crossed her face.

'Will I see you tomorrow?' he asked and wondered why her hair was softer and longer than his own. Black mother, white father, he thought. She nodded and burst out laughing as the car moved away. He had won her heart. Excitement ran through her body. She wanted him; how she wanted him. He would not be told of Toekies and Griet nor of her uncle Gaap. She would surely lose the Joster if her secrets were revealed. Had love finally come? The English-speaking coloured man she had submitted to at the tiny Kammagas motel had given her five pounds. Five pounds and twin girls. A heavy price for two nights of sex. Her people at Gamka had gossiped when the bulge became visible. Her uncle was angry at first but when she brought home the twins, there was joy and revelry. Sheep were slaughtered and the white man's liquor was shared and enjoyed by everyone. The girls were named after two women whom the shepherd had loved in his youth.

The first stranger had paid for the warmth of her body, but this one had won her heart, Talaah had told herself. One week after that meeting, Talaah and the Joster eloped to Cape Town where he was employed as a school teacher. The secret of the twins and her uncle was never revealed to anyone. Gaap had been confused and angered by her conduct but he had suffered in silence. He had lost Manga who had gone missing for many months only to return to Gamka carrying the child of Teens Boersma whose father Dirk owned the largest sheep and cattle-breeding farm in all of Kammagas. Gaap had loathed the young and arrogant Teens, but had accepted with some disquiet the food, money and furniture that Manga brought home.

There have always been prices to be paid for the safe-keeping of secrets, particularly those secrets that alienated men and women from the white tribe.

But from the simple people of Gamka no secrets could be hidden. They spoke openly about his sister's relationship with the brash Afrikaner. An argument between Gaap and Manga had ensued and he had hit her. She left the village and after several months of absence, she returned with Talaah. During that year his sister died leaving the child in his care. A child who had fled and deserted her own children. Eight long years had passed. Years which also reopened the pain of Manga's tragic death. But he had persevered and laboured hard to feed, clothe and educate the twins. The wounds healed partially with the passage of time. Now eight years since their birth — and still no word from her — he raised the girls with strict discipline and yet with a tenderness and concern that made the three of them inseparable.

... Time can be kind. It can cool the brain of its fever and empty the heart of bitterness and pain. Time is a practitioner that offers no pills nor tranquillisers. Only a balm and poultice of wind and sun and the changing of days that come to mend and rekindle the weak and pining spirit ... .

Gaap could not forget Talaah. He often took the twins to the highest mountain peak where he would point towards the distant horizon where the sun made its bed. Then pressing them close to his body, he would say: 'There, there in that place where the sun falls into its cradle like a baby, and the winds sings a Khoikhoi and San lullaby; in that country lives your mother Talaah and her mother Manga who is also my sister.'

'Is our mother beautiful?' asked the restless and inquisitive Toekies.

'Yes,' came the reply, 'soft and beautiful like the little lamb that sucks on its mother. Her hair is just like yours only curlier and browner.'

'And Manga her mother, what kind of woman is she?'

Griet's question saddened him a tiny bit but remembering it was not the time or place for sadness, Gaap laughed and said: 'Oh Manga! She is like the moon up there — round and full with the eyes and the temper of the mountain cat that kills the sheep and the goats.'

'Will we ever see our mother again?'

'Yes.' But deep in his heart he doubted his own words. He rubbed their heads gently and repeated his answer. But why, why had he spoken of Talaah and his Manga in the present tense as if they were alive? Both were dead; Manga in the grave of sand and stone, and Talaah in the grave of his heart.

'Oupa, sing to us that song which puts the sun to sleep,'

pleaded Toekies. Her tiny hands tugged at the shepherd's torn shirt, and she rubbed her head against his body. Gaap smiled. The song had been a family favourite for many, many generations.

> Biesie, biesie baamaa
> Hou djou baba saamaa
> Biesie, biesie baamaa
> Hoo' hoe sing haa mama
> Biesie, biesie baamaa
> Hou djou handjies saamaa
> Amen ...

Whenever he sang that lullaby, the twins would snuggle even closer to feel the sharp odour of his sweat reach deep into their nostrils. Sharp and warm like his watchful eyes. How he had sworn to hurt their mother for having deserted them, and for reopening his wounds. Wounds which had taken so long to heal. Manga was gone. And so was Talaah. Yet he had kept alive their names to the twins.

Then at twilight — when peace and a tranquil hush descended on Bushmanland, and certain animals and insects with their sounds and noises surrendered to the nocturnal creatures and plants — the shepherd and the twins would trudge towards their shack to sleep and dream. 'Biesie biesie baamaa, hoo' hoe sing haa' mama. Biesie biesie baamaa, hou djou handjies saamaa. Amen.'

Toekies, the frailer of the two, contracted a disease which baffled the doctors at the small Kammagas clinic. Mariette Huisamen, head of the medical services, arranged for the child to be transferred to Cape Town. She asked Gaap to bring Griet for tests. The shepherd was like a madman rushing about packing this and that, and then unpacking everything again. He had no fine clothes except the oversized black dinner jacket.

Mariette laughed when she saw him wearing the jacket with a well-worn hat tilted to one side. She thought to herself: What a comic the old man is and yet deeply pensive and obstinate at the same time. She had heard many tales about him. About his ability to cure sickness and even exorcise evil spirits. Some whites had told her about the inflammatory stories he related to the children. Stories which had turned the young 'Boesmans and Hotnots' into cheeky 'korrelkoppe'. Yet many of the older Afrikaners spoke of Gaap with respect.

Mariette, tall and imposing with brown hair, put her bag into the boot of the car. From there she scanned the back of the old man's head as if to read his thoughts. How a man that age could be so physically and spiritually strong was beyond her. At forty she was tired and listless. She used her work to keep her occupied and, in a strange way, to win the acknowledgement she sadly did not receive from her husband. Standing beside her car, she looked back briefly on her youth and the people who had mattered most in her life — her parents and two sisters who left Kammagas to live in South West Africa. There was a man she still loved though he had rejected her. A man who no longer found satisfaction in her body. Should she return to this place, this dry and desolate area and to these people? These fawning creatures whose only pleasure is sex? How much longer would she have to work among them?

Mariette drove in silence. Her thoughts moved to the child in the ambulance. Would the poor thing die? For all her years as a doctor none of her black patients had died from their sicknesses — at least not to her knowledge. Perhaps, away from their ramshacle clinic or in some quiet corner, some of them had sat huddled and coughed blood. Then the deep slumber — never to awaken again. Mariette sighed so loudly that Gaap lifted his head to look at her.

What kind of person — 'witmens' — is she to care so much about his little Toekies? Why was she respected by his people to the point of open adulation? Why did they do chores for her and give her presents and charms that were prized heirlooms? He had known many *witmense* in his seventy two years on earth but this tall woman with her sad troubled eyes, was not like the others.

The car jerked as Marietta changed gear to avoid hitting a man on the road. She pressed the hooter, both in greeting and as a warning. The man jumped to one side and waved excitedly.

These people, thought Mariette.

Mariette opened the car window to feel the crisp morning air refresh her face and enliven her spirits for the journey that lay ahead. Would the child they called Toekies be alive when they arrived in Cape Town? The face of her only child Antoinette, a child by her first marriage, flashed through her mind like the trees on the side of the untarred road. Would she ever see her daughter again? Why had life been so cruel to her? Where had she sinned or was it punishment for her ealier indifference to human suffering — and the reason why she had become a doctor? Why had her parents not informed her about how other people — especially the 'natives' and these 'boesmans' lived? It was during this self-interrogation that Griet asked her to stop the car. 'Ek will asseblief pee. Ek kan nie langer inhou nie,' Griet said shyly.

She watched Gaap take the child to a spot near a cluster of trees. The old man's stride was brisk and sure — a sign that he knew the terrain. Mariette was puzzled by her own curiosity and her admiration for him — however veiled these had been since she met him. Griet shuddered slightly as the warm liquid rushed through her to rain on to some ants that were dragging a dead fly to their hole. Her eyes fixed on the insects in wonderment.

'Oupa?' she asked, 'waarheen gaan die miere? Het hulle ook huise nes ons? Skyn die son ook vir hulle?' Her questions, which came rapidly, evoked a loud burst of laughter from her great-uncle. So loud that Mariette, waiting patiently in the car, wondered what they were doing. Without anwering Gaap lifted the child and still laughing quietly, he carried her to the car. A curious Mariette eyed them in the rear-view mirror as they resumed their journey.

They suffer and they laugh, thought Mariette.

As a high school pupil she had read about malnutrition and other related diseases. About the high mortality rate among 'these people' — these poor creatures who coughed and vomited until nothing was left of their lungs. These things she had read about but never dared or cared to find out. It was only when she entered medical school that the ills of the underprivileged really dawned on her. Mariette shuddered at her thoughts and wondered what it was that made people afraid and indifferent to the suffering of others — especially those who were outside one's own family or tribe.

Why had she not cared enough, why?

Perhaps the answer — like most issues among her people and those of her own class — lay deeply embedded in their history and in the traditions of the Afrikaner people. Perhaps this was why the 'naturelle' — the natives — and the 'boesmans' were treated by some white people as subhuman. Her thoughts raced with the wheels of the car. She adjusted her rear-view mirror and stared at Gaap and the child on his lap. She herself had been raised and cared for by one of these people — a woman who had been more than a mother to her. Still they remained a mystery to her. And then that little girl in the ambulance ahead of them — sweating and panting like an animal. And this quiet old man with his strong eyes that appeared always to be on fire. How he had stared at her when she urged him to allow the sick child to be taken to Cape Town.

'I will cure her! I will cure her!' he had screamed, holding Toekies in an iron grip. He was subdued and the child was placed in the ambulance. She had offered Gaap and little Griet a ride in her car rather than leave them behind. Mariette felt personally responsible though she could not explain why. She looked at Gaap again in the mirror. His eyes were moist and his fingers played through Griet's plaited hair. She envied him. Her first husband had run away taking with him their only daughter; a child she had not seen for eighteen years. A second marriage failed to produce any children and her present husband had threatened to leave. So many doctors, so many tests and still no child. How unfair God was — how brutally unfair life had become.

The silence became stifling.

'Wat is jou naam, outah?' she asked, hoping that by divulging his name he would also reveal something of his life. But Gaap did not speak. For to answer was not to know his place, or so the white man had said. She repeated her question and added that she needed to know only as a matter of course. Gaap nodded and disclosed his name. It was not long before Mariette learned the story of Manga, Talaah and the twins. Nobody had helped except the Man who lived in the mountains. The Man who always listened to his lamentations. This same Man, he told her, would not desert his Toekies.

'I hope not,' replied Mariette cynically, 'I've spoken to him many times over the years but he doesn't seem to hear me.'

The ambulance ahead of her sped faster, raising clouds of dust. The ride to Cape Town was long and tedious, and aggravated by the fact that her car was old and in disrepair. She would demand a new car on her return to Kammagas. Those days of working for peanuts and charity would be over. A new car or she would quit. If she went back ....

Several doctors attended to Toekies whose condition had deteriorated. She had lost consciousness in the ambulance. Mariette placed Gaap and Griet in an adjoining ward and explained her role and concern to a senior doctor. After several hours of tests she was informed that the child was not responding to treatment and that they feared for her life. Mariette felt pangs of guilt and remorse that she had not done her best for the child. 'Please God don't let her die. Please God, please,' she prayed aloud. Her public plea brought her to realise how personal her involvement had become. She could have remained at Kammagas to sort out her life — to try and patch things up with her husband and even entice him back into her bed. She thought of Gaap and Griet, how could she tell them that the doctors had little hope? Where was that Man of the mountain now? Why should the child have to die? Mariette slumped into a chair. She was tired. The long journey had taken its toll and she cried from the emotional stress.

The short young smooth-faced doctor whose black-rimmed spectacles made him look older than his forty-five years, touched her shoulders gently. 'Go and rest doctor,' he ordered. 'All is not lost.' His breath touched her face. Mariette looked up at him and nodded. His words reached inside of her — in that place where all feeling appeared to have died, giving her the warmth and comfort she had always longed for but could not get from her querulous husband. He had isolated himself and found pleasure and refuge in the bottle. Mariette knew she was losing him in the same way that she had lost patience in herself and in God. And here was this gentle and caring doctor whose words soothed her pain. Go and rest, he said. Where had she heard those words before? Why was there no happiness in her life when she gave so much to others? Mariette became deeply distraught and threw herself on an empty bed in another ward. She sobbed quietly and fell asleep. She was awakened by the kind doctor.

'Come quick! The child's condition has worsened. I'm afraid it's bad.' He took her hand into his as she jumped to her feet. Gaap and Griet looked on in silence as Mariette touched the sick child's shivering hand. A young doctor instructed the nurses to remove the shepherd and little Griet. 'Get them out. We can't have these people standing around!'

'No,' Mariette said, 'they are with me. They are my people.' The kind doctor smiled and pressed her hand firmly. His eyes were full of empathy and understanding. 'It's all right' he said 'they came with Dr Huisamen.'

'They are my people ....' The words echoed in Mariette's mind and made her feel good. Toekies was motionless but for heavy breathing. She mumbled incoherently.

Mariette put her hand on the old man's shoulder. 'Kyk outah, jou Toekies is baie, baie siek. Die dokters probeer hard. Alles is nou in die Here se hande.' Gaap's eyes blinked and he pressed Griet's hand. He suddenly lunged forward and grabbed the sick child and shouted: 'Shee my keend! Shee my Toekies!' He ran out of the ward holding the child to his chest. Griet ran behind him screaming and crying. Mariette tried to block him but she was bumped aside and fell against a huge bottle which crashed to the floor. Pandemonium broke out as the doctors and nurses chased after Gaap. The kind doctor ran to Mariette's aid. She cried bitterly — out of anger and pain. He lifted her into his arms. The heat of his breath reached into her face and her weeping subsided.

It seemed ages ago that she was embraced and comforted by a man. And now this gentle stranger took her into his arms. Her hunger for love and her desire to be touched and cared for, overwhelmed Mariette and she cried afresh. The embrace became stronger, more fervent. His eyes explored her face. He used his cheek to wipe her tears. 'Hush doctor, I'm here. I'm here,' he whispered. He knew that he was attracted to the tall woman from the moment he first saw her. The wedding band on her finger would not deter his feelings. How ringed and deep were her eyes — so full of pain and loneliness. His arms locked around her shoulders and he pacified her. They returned to the ward and he urged her to lie down.

Mariette put her head on the pillow and sobbed. The loud screeching of a car came from outside. People screamed and shouted at the top of their voices. Mariette got up and ran out of the ward. The doctor followed. 'Wait doctor, wait!' he called out as she passed through the huge swinging doors. He heard Mariette scream. When he got outside, he found her bending over the old man's body. Griet cried hysterically. Gaap and Toekies were dead. Their mangled bodies lay apart in pools of blood. Mariette cried bitterly as she lifted the dead child on to her lap. The kind doctor took Griet into his arms and stroked her head. His hand rested gently on Mariette's shoulder. He knew in his heart that amid all that pain and sorrow and death, he had found love. He had never loved a woman before but this time it was different. Mariette would be his....

It was nightfall in Gamka.

Gaap the storyteller and shepherd was buried beside the plants. The wind rolled restlessly over his grave — to and fro; pining. A melancholy sound came from the arid lands beyond the mountain range and drifted towards the empty shack where the old man and his family had lived. The sound drifted toward the place where the yellow flames once danced and shone in the eyes of the inquisitive children of Gamka who came to listen to the tales of the glory and the subjugation of the San and the Khoikhoi.

All was quiet but for the wind; the wailing and pining wind that rolled restlessly over Gaap's grave — back and forth; to and fro. . . .

Xai-Xai, the curious, and the bravest among all the boys of Gamka, stirred in his bed. He had loved the storyteller and was deeply affected by his death. But although his Taa-Gaap had taken much wisdom with him to the grave, he, Xai-Xai would always remember the folktales and history of his people. Someday he would take the place of the old man. The children would also sit near him by the fireside, and he too would take the snuff and then wipe the eyes quietly and secretively so that no-one might know he was crying.

The boy covered himself with a thick blanket and once outside in the cold, he walked towards Gaap's shack. He entered and saw that everything inside it — as he knew it — had changed. Toekies was gone. Griet had gone to live with the white doctor. He shivered and wrapped himself up more securely against the cold night air. Yes, things had changed inside the desolate shack. But the world outside — the trees and the shrubs and the mountains had not changed. Everything was as it had been. The moon and the stars there, as they had been thousands of years ago. And the sun would rise again; sure and strong as ever. Xai-Xai walked towards the foot of Gaap's favourite mountain. The Presence was there like the throbbing inside his chest. It was the same strength he had seen and felt in the storyteller's eyes and in the firm but gentle hands. Mighty. Confident. Reassuring. And it was calling him, calling him.

And the boy would continue to relate the story of his people to the young — only he would have one more tragic tale to tell; that of the storyteller shepherd before him. He ascended the mountain and went to the place where his Taa-Gaap used to sit and talk to the Man who listened to him. There was no chill in the air. Instead a strange, inexplicable warmth descended on Xai-Xai. The sadness which he had carried with him to and from the burial service was gone.

A new hope filled his heart. Gaap, the fountain and fire of his strength — his guiding star — was with him on the mountain.

Tomorrow he, Xai-Xai the faithful and the dauntless, will tell stories of the San and the Khoikhoi who once ruled the earth and spoke to the insects and the animals. Long before the Jackals came.

... And if you ever doubted the existence of God, then go to the place called Bushmanland near Namaqualand, which lies far, far into the north-western Cape near South West Africa, and some miles from Botswana. God lives there. Ever-present and austere. Patient with all that He created. Listening and brooding over the vast expanse where flat trees and thorny bushes and shrubs bow in deference. There, only man is a foolish and vain and stubborn and forgetful creature. Only man.

AFRIKA ROAD

Where are many roads and lanes and streets and byways in South Africa but none quite like me, Afrika Road.

Each black township, no matter where it is situated, has an Afrika Road of its own. We are commonly known as 'The Tar Road', and those who create the townships and make the laws also conceive roads like us to facilitate the easy mobility of military and police vehicles. Usually there is a single road into and out of the townships. But the black people say they are not fools. They know the real motives of the rulers.

I am long and black and beautiful like a flat piece of liquorice. Some folks say that my beauty has been spoiled by the obstinate white line because it cuts into my melanic majesty. But the line, like the Law of the land, slithers defiantly from the sun's bedroom in the west where I begin, to Masphala Hill in the east — a hotseat of conferred power which houses the Bantu Council Chambers and the police station.

I, Afrika Road, know and have endured the weight and pressure of all sorts of moving objects: human, animal and mechanical. I groaned under the grinding repression of many military convoys and police brass bands that led the mayoral processions to the Hill of power. I also witness weddings and childbirths, and hear the noise of speeding police cars and ambulances, as well as the plaintive burial dirges of people weeping mournfully as they go. I hear the cries of the lonely of heart and I am familiar with the bustling din of jubilant folk whose merriment and laughter permeate the ghetto.

I am a mighty road.

All the dusty and soil-eroded lanes and streets converge on my body, bringing throngs of panting people. And I hold them all on my sturdy lap, year in and year out; birth in and death out.

There was a time when I was a teeming cauldron of 'people

on the boil'. The flames of mob anger and violence had razed the homes and businesses of men and women who threw in their lot and collaborated with the rulers of the land, or so the people said. Policemen and suspected informers and agents were brutally attacked. Some were even put to the torch. Yet amid the fear and frenzy of the marching and shouting masses, I, Afrika Road, caught glimpses of genuine gaiety on the people's faces. It was a welcome paradox nonetheless. Humour and anger marching side-by-side.

That day the marchers varied in shade between chocolate brown and shining ebony and fair apricot-skinned activists — rich characteristics for the human centipede that took to the streets.

It was one of many dates anywhere on the calendar of black resistance. The masses had heaved and swayed and breathed in the wild wind of their own passions. Occasionally the main body of the crowd opened up its floodgates and swallowed several hundreds of new protesters and their assortment of crude weaponry: sticks, stones, axes, home-made swords, knives and dustbin lids. Four hundred people poured out of Mpanza Street; five hundred from Matambo and a half-drunk dozen from Sis Sonti's shebeen. The call to arms had a magnetic pull even for the imbibers. A soldier was a soldier drunk or sober, or so the leaders said. What mattered most were numbers.

Between Goba and Zamani streets, where the élite owner-built homes stand proud and indifferent, only three youngsters joined the swelling ranks. The Mkhuku Shanty Town dwellers mingled eagerly in their hundreds. The march gained momentum. Men, women, children and the fire-eating T-shirted comrades — soldiers without uniforms or conventional armoury, were carried along the hard journey of insurrection, aware that death waited for them on Masphala Hill.

And they sang defiantly.

Songs that challenged and mocked the armed keepers of the Hill; that hated Hill which many blacks see as one of countless links in the chain of bondage and humiliation, or so the people said. Those who served in State-created institutions and sought and found sanctuary inside the high barbed-wire walls of the Hill, were branded puppets, sellouts and 'mpimpi' — the word used to describe informers and fifth-columnists.

I, Afrika Road, bore that maddened crowd as it rambled and swayed in the fervour of revolt towards the Hill of confrontation where hundreds of heavily-armed battalions of soldiers, policemen and the local 'greenbean' law enforcers kept vigil. Their automatic weapons caught flashes of the shimmering gold and orange sunrays that blistered from a cloudless sky. The singing reached fever pitch when a group of chanting, flag-carrying militant youth took the lead towards the waiting death-machine.

The songs spoke of imminent battle and vengeance, and of the people's hunger for liberation. Songs which exhorted the Bothas to release Nelson Mandela and all the other political prisoners. There were martial strophes which alluded to the impending acquisition of AK47s, Scorpion automatic pistols and bazooka rocket launchers. Then came the electrifying toi-toi war dance which appeared to penetrate and possess the very souls of the marchers. It seemed to me that the masses yearned to touch the faces of death or victory — whichever came first.

The toi-toi is a ritual dance which people have come to fear and hate or love and revere depending on which side of the political trenches a person stood — with the masses or the 'masters'.

A truly awe-inspiring sight, thousands of angry and anxious feet in an exuberant display of bravado and daring. Up and down, back and forth; then forward and ever onward — spilling the froth and sweat of excitement on my black brow.

And I, Afrika Road, saw schoolchildren in khaki uniforms raise their wooden guns at the law enforcers on the Hill. Bullets made of hot breath and noise and spit, reverberated in the air. 'We are going to kill them in the company of their children,' the khaki-clad warriors chanted. Death waited for them on the Hill as the crowd drew closer and closer. It would be the final confrontation: more than sixty thousand marchers heading for the showdown. Heading for freedom, or so they said.

You see it in their youthful eyes: a readiness to feel the familiar thud on the chest, and to hear the cracking of bone and the ripping of lung as the fire-power of the law enforcers makes its forced entry and exit through the dark dissident flesh.

You see it in the flailing young arms of the children — always the children in the firing line — in tattered clothes or in school uniforms; T-shirted or naked chests; you see their hands fisted in the ardour of transient emotions; lives destined never to fully experience the essence of a natural childhood. You see them.

And I, Afrika Road, have seen them rise and then run undaunted against the ill wind; falling but emerging anew through sheaves of resisting corn — giving the earth life that genuine life might be reborn — or so I have heard the people's poets say during the many long marches.

A late model car zoomed out of a small, nondescript lane between Zwide and Zwane streets. The well-dressed, well-fed driver, a wealthy local businessman and Bantu councillor, was en route to his sanctuary on Masphala Hill. He swerved noisily on to me. People dived to safety as the expensive imported vehicle screeched, skidded and smoked at the wheels, and burned me.

Someone shouted 'Mpimpi!'

The human telegraph wire relayed the hated word and echoed it against the blue sky. The leaders in front got the message, stopped and gave their backs to the waiting militia, who instinctively raised their guns at the ready in anticipation of attack.

The laminated windows of the car sagged under the weight of flying rock. Some of the youngsters jumped on it and smashed the front windscreen. The terror-stricken man sat open-mouthed, immobilised by his fear of death.

And I, Afrika Road, watched; knowing the fateful outcome. I have witnessed it too many times.

'Mpimpi!'

The chilling indictment rang out one final time.

A huge stone crushed the driver's skull. His eyes blinked and then went blank. Blood poured from his ears, nose and mouth. They dragged him out. The back of his head cracked against me. I drank his blood just like I tasted the blood of many before him, and many more to come.

It is the law and the legacy.

Someone rolled a tyre. Someone lifted a petrol can. Someone struck a match on Afrika Road . . . .